THE MEDALLION OF TIBEN

Judy Levering-Duff

Outskirts Press
Denver, Colorado

Outskirts Press
http://www.outskirtspress.com

ISBN: 0-9725874-9-7

Outskirts Press and the "OP" logo are trademarks belonging to
Outskirts Press, Inc.

Printed in the United States of America

To Uncle Dan,

You shared your faith,
your stories,
your love of nature, education, and adventure with us all.
May we teach our children all that you taught us.

A very special thanks-

I have had such wonderful support from so many people since I starting writing my books. I want to acknowledge all those who have helped to make my dream come true.

First, last, and always, I want to thank the loves of my life-my husband Jack and my daughters Jacklyn, Caitlin, Amanda, and Mariah. Thank you for putting up with my craziness and for being the best promotional team in the business.

Secondly, I want to thank all the family members and friends who have been behind me all the way. Your support and love has meant the world to me.

I also would like to thank two people who have been kind enough to read my first drafts and tell me if I should continue or use the shredder. To Melanie Heller and Meghan Maguire-much love from Mama Duff.

A big thank you to Debra for the great job you do and for doing your job with class and kindness.

And last but never least, thank you to Chris, Brent, Jeanine and everyone else at Outskirts Press for their professionalism, support, vision, and hard work. You are all a pleasure to work with.

THE MEDALLION OF TIBEN

Judy Levering-Duff

Chapter One

In Sickness and in Health

Princess Isabella allowed her nurses one last minute to fuss with her hair and clothing, then sent them away. She twirled in front of the mirror, her golden gown billowing out around her feet, as a few strands slipped from the hairdo her nurses had created. Leaning close to the mirror, she examined the tiny crescent-shaped scar on her nose. With a last twirl, she left her bedroom and headed toward the throne room.

After ten years of only being allowed to sit on a throne in a glass room, Princess Isabella had enjoyed the past six months of freedom. She could now play in the garden with the other children, and her friend Phinius Squallem was teaching her all the things she had never been allowed to learn.

Today she was speaking before a group of her father's advisers, describing her kidnapping, her journey back home to the Kingdom of Grom, and all the interesting creatures she had met.

At first her parents, King Oscar and Queen Louisa, hadn't wanted her to tell anyone what had happened while she was away. She had been nervous and exhausted when she explained her experiences to them, so her words hadn't made much sense. Her parents were afraid others would think her mind had been damaged and would pity her. She tried again to tell them after she was rested and able to explain more clearly, but by then they refused to discuss it. They wanted to forget that it had ever happened. It was days before her friend Lyalus convinced them to let her explain exactly what had happened; then they understood how much she had been through and how strong she had to be just to survive. Once they heard the whole story, they were proud of her and wanted others to hear about her achievements.

Walking down the corridor, Isabella thought back on all that she had been through. When she was born, she was so perfectly beautiful her parents built a special glass room where she was put on display for all the people of the kingdom to see. Her father decreed that she was to be pampered and protected so nothing would ruin her extraordinary loveliness. Twenty-four hours a day, she was waited on hand and foot, and her only duty was to sit on her throne for the crowds of people to enjoy. She wasn't allowed to play or be around other children, and no one taught her anything except the proper way to sit while she was being admired.

Isabella reached the throne room and made her way to the front. The whole kingdom had been in an uproar when the princess disappeared, and now the room was full of people waiting to hear how she had survived her ordeal.

"Good afternoon, ladies and gentlemen. I am Princess Isabella of Grom. Nine months ago, an evil troll named Malachi stole me from my throne and carried me off to his cave. He locked me in a cage and kept me there for three weeks. He kidnapped me so he could enjoy my beauty without sharing me with others. After a few days in the cage, I became dirty and my gown became torn. Once I was no longer perfect, instead of staring at me, he had me help him mix his potions. Malachi had magical powers and made potions from roots and herbs. He taught me many things. He taught me colors, measurements, how to build a fire, which roots and berries were safe to eat, and how to trap animals for food."

"Eventually, I escaped from Malachi and set out to find my way home. Although it was Malachi's fault that I was alone in the wilderness, it's also true that without the things he taught me, I probably would've died." A few of the more sensitive females dabbed at their eyes with lace hankies.

Isabella swallowed a grin and continued. "On my journey, I met many interesting creatures. First, I came upon a whole village that lives inside a mountain. They called their home The Garden of Robyia, and they called themselves Lanolions. They were friendly once they got to know me, but they aren't used to outsiders because they never leave their home inside the mountain. The Lanolions are short, squat beings with horns, yellow eyes, and lots of toes, yet they think anyone who doesn't look like them is ugly. They were repulsed by my appearance." There were murmurs of disbelief by the crowd who had admired her beauty for years.

When all was silent, Isabella said, "I also met a tribe of monkey-people called Gorilmen. They live in the treetops and hold trespassers captive. The captives must entertain the tribe in some way in order to earn their freedom. I stayed with them for several days before they set me free." Isabella remembered how much the Gorilmen laughed at her simple trick of shooting water out of her mouth.

"Then I met Phinius Squallem. Phinius was a hermit who had been abused as a child because the chief of his tribe resented the fact that

Phinius could read and write. Once Phinius realized how much he was missing, he decided to come out of hiding and traveled from village to village teaching anyone with a desire to learn. As many of you know, Phinius now teaches the children of the kingdom, including me." Isabella paused to make sure her audience was still interested. They were hanging on every word.

Isabella enjoyed describing Grammy, a friendly old woman who took her in and sewed some clothes to replace the ragged gown Isabella had been wearing. Grammy lived in the woods with only her pet bird Orion to keep her company. Isabella and Grammy had managed to communicate, despite the fact Grammy used some of the strangest words Isabella had ever heard.

There were plenty of smiles as Isabella told the crowd about the Kingdom of Sowden, a palace she had thought was her own at first. The royal family, King Hamlet, Queen Hogalynn, Princess Hogitha, Princess Pigetta, Princess Porcellina, and Princess Porkita had treated her like a member of the family. Despite their snouts, pink skin, and curly tails, Isabella found them to be very much like her own family.

"I left Sowden with Mystic, a one-horned magical creature who led me to the village of Teoli. The people of Teoli chose a young warrior named Lyalus to take me the rest of the way home. But on our journey, a giant hairy beast attacked us and Lyalus was injured." The audience held their breath as Isabella described the way she outwitted the beast to save Lyalus.

"When I finally arrived home, as happy as I was to see my parents again, I knew I didn't want to spend my days sitting in the glass room anymore." Isabella told the crowd how much her life had changed since her return. It had taken some doing, but she had finally convinced her father that she had other strengths and talents besides her beauty. Once he was convinced, he allowed her to leave her glass room and lead a freer life. Now that she was able to spend more time with her parents, their relationship had grown much closer.

The advisers were permitted to ask Isabella a few questions at the end of her talk, which she answered honestly. Then her guards escorted her to the dining room where her parents waited to share the midday meal.

"Good afternoon, Mother, Father. Sorry to keep you waiting," Isabella said as she gave each of her parents a quick hug.

"Hello, darling. How did your talk with the council go?" asked the Queen.

"Fine. I think they were shocked by some of the things I told them, but they seemed very interested in learning about all the different creatures I met on my journey."

"I had hoped they would be," admitted the King. "I have some good news for you, Isabella."

"Yes, Father?"

"A rider arrived today with a message. It was from the Kingdom of Sowden. It seems Princess Hogitha is to be married, and we are invited to attend the wedding!"

"Can we go? Please, Father?"

"Absolutely. I have been looking forward to meeting them. I wish they could have accepted the invitation we extended last month after our guards located their palace, but I am glad we are to meet at last. I want to thank them for welcoming you into their home and all the help they gave you."

Isabella was squirming with excitement. "I can't believe it! Hogitha is getting married, and I'm going to see Porkita again!"

The family spent the rest of the meal discussing the upcoming trip to Sowden. Each was excited not only about seeing the royals, but also about taking their first family trip together.

They planned to leave in six days. It would take them two days to travel to Sowden and then they would have several days to visit with their hosts before the wedding. The King was making arrangements for an escort of guards, and the Queen was busy selecting gifts for the royal family. When Isabella told Phinius about the trip and told him that they would be gone for two weeks, he came up with a plan of his own.

7

"I believe I will ask your father's permission to leave the kingdom while you are away," stated the old man. "I want to check on some of the villages and see if the teachers I sent them are working out."

"I'm sure Father won't mind. It was generous of you to agree to come here and teach us in the first place. You have taught us so much these past six months. I hope everything is going well in the villages. If you go to Teoli, would you say hello to Lyalus and his parents for me?"

"I plan to make Teoli my first stop. I will give young Lyalus and his family your regards," Phinius assured her.

The King thought that Phinius's idea to visit the villages was a good one. He offered to send an escort with Phinius, but the old teacher declined. He told the King he was sure he would have no trouble traveling on his own. Phinius arranged to leave the day before the King, Queen, and Isabella were to leave.

Isabella woke early on the morning Phinius was to depart so she could say good-bye. After seeing Phinius off, she hurried to join her parents in the dining room for breakfast.

"Is there something wrong?" Isabella asked as she took her seat, surprised by their grim expressions.

The King answered, "Nothing for you to worry about, Isabella."

Isabella sighed. "Father, I thought you were through pampering me. If there's something wrong, I'd like to help."

The King rubbed his temples before answering, "I wasn't trying to leave you out, Isabella. I just didn't want you to worry. A number of people in the kingdom have fallen ill. There is nothing you can do to help. Our medical advisers are taking care of everything."

Isabella spent the morning working on her reading and writing and forgot about the people who were ill until the King didn't show up for lunch.

"Won't Father be joining us?"

The Queen hesitated and then told her, "Father is talking with the medical advisers. I'm afraid more people have fallen ill. Your father and I are both very concerned."

"What kind of sickness is it? Can't the medical advisers make them well?"

"That's the problem. More and more people are getting sick and the advisers don't know what is causing it," answered the Queen.

Isabella was in her room that afternoon helping her nurses pack her belongings for the trip to Sowden when her parents entered. Her father looked worn and haggard. Her mother was wringing her hands.

"Leave us, please," her father directed the nurses. Isabella sank down on the edge of the bed. She could tell by her parents' expressions that the news wasn't good.

"Isabella," her father began, "we have a bit of a crisis. The illness is spreading quickly. We can't figure out what is making the people ill, so we can't stop others from becoming ill, and we can't help those who are already suffering."

"Is there anything I can do to help, Father?"

"There *is* something you can do, Isabella, but I'm afraid you won't like it," answered the King. "Your mother and I feel we should be here to help in any way we can. We wouldn't be comfortable leaving the kingdom to attend a wedding when so many of our subjects are ill and more are becoming so."

Isabella swallowed hard before answering, "So we aren't going to the Kingdom of Sowden. That's all right, I understand."

The King and Queen exchanged glances. The Queen took Isabella's hand and said, "Your father and I feel *we* should be here, but we don't want *you* to be here where you could become ill. We want you to go on without us and—"

Isabella protested, "No! I don't want to go without you and Father! I'll stay here with you. Maybe I can help!"

"No, Isabella," her mother replied, "we won't argue about this. You are leaving tomorrow with an escort of guards. They will deliver you safely to Sowden and then come back to escort us. You will only be away from us for a few days. You will be safer away from here for now."

"But I don't want to go without you! Why can't I—"

"Isabella," the King ordered, "you heard your mother. You will leave in the morning." He softened his voice and coaxed, "Your mother and I will be there with you before you know it. In the meantime, you will be safe with Porkita and her family. You'll have a lot of fun! We'll take care of the problem here and then we can relax and enjoy the wedding with you, all right?"

Isabella nodded reluctantly.

"Good girl," said her father. "Now you finish your packing and the three of us will have a nice dinner together. A farewell dinner! How does that sound?"

Isabella managed a weak smile and started gathering the clothes that were laid out on the bed. Her back was to her parents, so they didn't see the tears gathering in her eyes.

Isabella rose early the next morning and put on the clothes her nurses had laid out. She entered the dining room to find her parents waiting. Grabbing a muffin and a goblet of juice, Isabella took her seat and began eating.

"Did you sleep well, darling?" her mother asked.

Isabella looked up at her mother to answer and was struck by how tired and pale she appeared.

"Mother, you don't look well! You're not sick, are you?"

"No, dear," the Queen was quick to reassure her. "I'm just tired. Your father and I were up all night trying to solve this crisis."

"I still think I should stay and . . ." Both her parents shook their heads and she gave up. Isabella finished her juice and her muffin, and then stood up.

"Well, then, I guess I'm ready to go." Isabella was afraid to look her parents in the eye. She was afraid she would start crying if she did. Her parents rose and guided her to where her royal escort waited. All her cases had already been loaded; all that remained was to say goodbye.

The King chose to go first. He took her in his arms and said, "Goodbye, my little princess. Have a safe journey. I will see you very soon. I love you, Isabella."

Isabella was too choked up to speak, so she buried her face in his robe and hugged him harder. Her mother pulled her from her father and into her own arms.

"Don't cry, darling. Everything will be okay. I hate to let you go like this when we just got you back, but there really is no other choice. I won't risk having you get sick like all the others. You will be safe with Porkita and her family, and Father and I will be there in a few days. Remember how much Father and I love you. Now go." Her mother guided her into the carriage.

As the horses pulled the carriage down the dirt lane leading away from the palace, Isabella leaned out the side and waved as hard as she could. Before long, the palace and her parents disappeared behind the cloud of dust kicked up by the horses' hooves.

It would be many weeks before she would see her parents again.

Chapter Two

Hog-tied

The ride to Sowden passed slowly for Isabella without her parents to keep her company. The guards stopped at regular intervals to allow Isabella to stretch her legs and have a bite to eat from the large baskets of food the palace cooks had provided. The rest of the time, Isabella studied the books Phinius had lent her or stared out the window at the scenery. Several times she thought she recognized landmarks from her previous journey, but it all passed by so quickly it was hard to be sure.

When it grew dark, they stopped beside a stream for the night. The guards fed and watered the horses; then they built a fire for light and warmth. Isabella tried to help set up the camp, but the guards insisted that she sit and let them take care of everything. She smiled as she thought about how different this journey was from the last one when she had to fend for herself. Sleeping under the stars on a feather-stuffed mat surrounded by soldiers was a far cry from the scared, lonely nights she had spent sleeping in the dirt.

The second day of the trip was more of the same until late afternoon when Isabella spied something on the horizon. It was still too far away for her to make out clearly, but from the size of it, she felt it had to be her friend Porkita's palace.

By the time they were close enough for her to be sure, she was too excited to sit still. Bouncing up and down on the seat with her head hanging out of the window, she strained her eyes for some sign of her hosts. As they approached the large gates, Isabella saw the front entrance of the big pink palace open. Porkita rushed out, followed more regally by the King, Queen, and the three other princesses. Isabella had a hard time waiting for the carriage to come to a complete stop before jumping out and running into her friend's outstretched arms.

"Isabella! Oh, Isabella, I'm so happy to see you!" squealed Porkita.

"I'm happy to see you too, Porkita. I thought we would never get here!"

King Hamlet stepped forward and snorted, "Humph! Isabella, my dear, it is good to see you safe and sound, but where are your parents?"

Isabella curtsied before the King, then responded, "They were detained by a problem in the kingdom, Your Majesty. They promised to arrive before the wedding, though."

"Since we have that settled, I think I deserve more than a curtsy, don't you?" he said with a twinkle in his eye. Isabella rushed forward to hug him. After giving her a good squeeze, he passed her to Queen Hogalynn's arms.

"Isabella, I was so worried about you, and so grateful when your soldiers arrived to tell us you were safely home. And now you are here with us again under happier circumstances! How well you look! You could still use some fattening up, though!" The Queen thought everyone should be as plump as she and her daughters.

Porkita's three older sisters came forward to embrace Isabella. Isabella congratulated Hogitha on her wedding and told her how excited she was to be in attendance. The family ushered Isabella into the palace dining room.

"We are having lots of feasts in the next few days to celebrate the wedding, but we thought it would be nice if it was just us tonight. Of course, we expected your parents to be here so we would be able to get to know them," added the Queen, gazing down her pink snout at Isabella. "But this will be just as nice. It will be like the last time you were here."

The dining table was groaning under the huge platters of food. This time Isabella was not surprised to see that the meal was made mostly of corn, the family's favorite food. There were corn pancakes, corn fritters, corn casseroles, corn muffins, corn pudding, and a variety of other fruits and vegetables. The family took their seats, with Isabella seated next to Porkita, and began the meal.

"What kind of crisis detained your parents, Isabella, if you are free to speak about it?" asked the King, filling his plate to overflowing.

"It was a strange illness that affected some of the people of the kingdom. The medical advisers have been trying to find out what is causing it, but they still hadn't figured it out when I left," answered Isabella.

"I hope they find the answer quickly," said the King, his mouth full of food. "It is most disheartening when your subjects have a problem and you can't solve it for them."

Most of the dinner conversation centered on Hogitha's wedding. Hogitha was anxious to share the details with Isabella. Guests were coming from all over. Feasts and dancing were planned for every evening leading up to the wedding, and Isabella was to be included in all of it.

"Fill your plate again, Hogitha dear," the Queen ordered. "You don't want to be skinny on your wedding day! Remember, you can never be too pink or too fat! Isabella, you must eat more than that!" She piled more on Isabella's plate.

Isabella smiled and took another bite. "What is your future husband's name, Hogitha?"

Hogitha finished off another ear of corn dripping with butter before answering, "His name is Prince Hogden of the Kingdom of Swinerick. He's wonderful!" Hogitha had a dreamy look on her face as she reached for a corn muffin. "He's the largest male in his kingdom. Nobody can grow as much corn in one season as Hogden, or eat as much either!"

"How did the two of you eat-I mean meet?" asked Isabella.

"It was so romantic! We were invited to a feast at his kingdom. I was at the buffet table, and I reached for a corn cake at the same time he did. Our hands touched, and we turned to look into each other's eyes. He pulled the corn cake toward him, and I pulled it toward me. He pulled harder. So did I. Finally, it broke in half. I shoved my half in my mouth, and he shoved his half in his mouth. As I watched him chew, with crumbs tumbling onto his royal robe, I knew I wanted to spend the rest of my life with him! We spent the whole evening eating and talking together; by our third dessert, we were in love!"

"It sounds--er--wonderful," responded Isabella, thinking it didn't sound at all romantic to her.

"The Queen and I are very pleased with Hogitha's choice of a husband," said the King. "Hogden is exactly the type husband we had hoped our daughters would marry."

"When will I meet him?" asked Isabella.

"Hogden and his whole family will be arriving the day before the wedding," answered the Queen. "More guests are arriving tomorrow and the feast tomorrow night will be huge. I do hope your parents will be here by then, Isabella."

"So do I, Your Majesty, so do I," said Isabella.

After dinner, Isabella and the family went into the parlor to talk and exchange news. Isabella told them about the rest of her journey, including her confrontation with the beast to save Lyalus. The family was shocked and saddened to hear all that she had gone through.

"I should have sent an escort of guards to go with you!" bellowed the King. "I thought you would be safe with Mystic. I thought once she took you to the villages, the rest of the way home would be easy for you."

"It wasn't your fault or Mystic's fault. Mystic took me to my friend Phinius and Phinius took me to Lyalus. Nobody could have known I wouldn't be safe with Lyalus. Lyalus tried to protect me. He saved me from the beast. Then the beast grabbed him. I could have left Lyalus and gone home safely, but I chose to put myself in danger to save him. It's my fault, no one else's."

The Queen pulled a cord hanging from the ceiling. Moments later, a servant came.

"Please bring us a large tray of sweets and some hot drinks," she requested. When the servant had left, she told the others, "All this talk of beasts and danger has made me nervous, and the only thing that calms me down is to eat."

Isabella tried to steer the conversation away from her adventure by asking the family what had been happening in their lives.

"Well, I have been falling in love and getting engaged," answered Hogitha.

"What about everyone else?" asked Isabella. "What's happening in your life, Pigetta?"

"Everything has changed since you were here, Isabella," Pigetta answered, "and it's all because of you. Now Father lets us do so many more things. We don't have to sit and have our beauty treatments all day anymore. We can walk in the gardens, have friends over to visit, and do lots of other fun activities."

"That's wonderful!" exclaimed Isabella. "I'm so happy for all of you!"

Porkita chimed in, "You haven't even heard the best part! Father has one of his advisers teaching us in the mornings! I'm learning to read!"

Isabella threw her arms around her chubby friend. "Oh, Porkita! That's the best news I've had in a long time!"

Hogitha snorted. "Well, personally, I think a wedding is much better news than learning to read silly old books." She looked offended as she picked up another sweet from the tray the servant had brought in and ate it in one bite.

Sorry to have hurt her feelings, Isabella put an arm around her broad shoulders and assured her, "Of course your wedding is the biggest news I've heard, Hogitha. It's thrilling news. I didn't mean to say that it wasn't. I was just happy for Porkita, that's all."

Brightening, Hogitha gave Isabella a quick hug and then helped herself to another sweet. "It's fine, Isabella. I'm happy for Porkita and her old books, too." Suddenly she squealed, "Ooh! This one has candied corn in it! Yummy! Do have one, Isabella."

Isabella smiled and said, "No, thank you, Hogitha. I ate so much dinner, I feel like I'm going to burst!"

The Queen protested, "Why, Isabella, you hardly ate anything! I must speak to your mother about your lack of appetite. It isn't an attractive quality in a princess. Princes expect their wives to be healthy eaters, you know. I always tell my girls to neglect your hair and nails if you must, but *never* neglect your figure." With a big smile, the Queen popped another sweet into her wide mouth.

Isabella turned away to hide her own smile and wondered what Queen Hogalynn would think when she saw how fit and trim Isabella's mother was.

The eating and talking continued until the Queen noticed Isabella hiding a yawn behind her fist.

"How selfish we have all been!" she admonished. "Here poor Isabella is exhausted from traveling all day, and we have kept her up with our silly chatter. Come child, we must get you to bed."

"No, really, I'm not that tired. It's so nice to sit here and talk with all of you again. As a matter of fact, I don't feel one bit tired," Isabella protested, but just then another yawn betrayed her.

"We'll have plenty of time to talk while you are here, Isabella," the Queen assured her. "Right now, we all need our beauty sleep. Come, girls, let's retire to our rooms. Isabella, would you like to stay with Porkita again, or would you prefer a room of your own?"

"Oh, no. I would really like to stay in Porkita's room, if you don't mind."

"Very well. Porkita, hurry along and get Isabella settled in your room. Goodnight, girls," the Queen said, giving each of them a sugary kiss on the cheek.

The King stood, stretched, and grunted. He gave each of his daughters and Isabella a kiss goodnight and then waddled tiredly from the room followed by the Queen. Porcellina, Hogitha, and Pigetta left next, and last to exit were Porkita and Isabella, hand in hand.

At breakfast the next morning, Isabella asked if she could spend some time with Mystic. The magical one-horned creature had become a good friend on Isabella's last trip when she escorted her from Sowden to the village where Phinius was staying.

"Mystic isn't at the palace right now, Isabella," the King informed her. "A week ago, she told me she had experienced one of her visions and needed to take a short trip to investigate something. I expected her to be back by now, but she hasn't returned. I'm sure she will be back in time for the wedding, though. You'll be able to visit with her then."

"Did she tell you what she saw in the vision?" Isabella asked.

"No. She just said she had to check something and then she would explain it all." The King looked puzzled, and said, "It *was* kind of strange, though. Mystic has never been secretive about anything before. She's usually so open and forthright."

When the family had finally finished eating, Porkita got up and whispered in her mother's ear. The Queen smiled and nodded. Porkita came back and took Isabella's hand and led her from the room. Once they were in the corridor, Isabella asked where they were going.

"I asked Mother if we could be excused. I thought it would be fun if you and I made a surprise gift for Hogitha and Hogden."

"That's a great idea, Porkita. But what kind of present? I don't know how to make anything, do you?"

"I can sew a little. Can you?"

"No. Not even a little."

"Can you draw?" asked Porkita.

"Not well."

"Neither can I," admitted Porkita.

"So what can we do?" asked Isabella.

Both girls thought for a moment. Then Isabella exclaimed, "I have an idea! You know how much Hogitha loves sweets? We could make some candies for her!"

"Make candy? Do you know how to make candy?" asked Porkita.

"No, but I'm sure it can't be that hard. The cooks would help us, wouldn't they?"

"I guess so. Let's go ask them."

Isabella and Porkita hurried downstairs to the kitchen. The cooks were bustling around preparing food for that evening's feast. Isabella tugged on the sleeve of one of the workers.

"Excuse me . . ."

The cook turned to face the two princesses and immediately dropped to a curtsy.

"Your Highnesses, you shouldn't be down here. If you need something, just ring and someone will bring you a tray."

"No, you don't understand. We aren't hungry, we—"

Porkita interrupted, "Actually, I could eat a little something."

Isabella frowned at her. "Not now, Porkita. We just had a big break-fast."

"But that was ages ago!" sighed Porkita.

"It was only a few minutes ago, Porkita!" Isabella turned her attention to the cook again. "We wanted to ask you a favor. We want to make some candies for Hogitha and Hogden as a wedding present but we need your help."

"Oh, aren't you girls sweet! I'll be happy to help you. What kind of treats do you want to make?" asked the cook.

"Well, she really likes the kind that has candied corn in the center. Can you teach us to make those?" asked Isabella.

"Certainly, Your Highness. When would you like to begin?"

"Can we do it now or are you too busy?" asked Isabella.

"Let me check with the head cook and see if I can help you now."

Isabella turned to speak to Porkita, but she was not there. Isabella looked around the kitchen and saw Porkita by one of the stoves. As Isabella watched, Porkita sniffed at the contents of several pots, then grabbed a spoon and started tasting the different concoctions. Isabella shook her head and walked over to where Porkita stood.

"Porkita! What are you doing?"

Porkita dropped the spoon and a guilty look crossed her face.

"I'm just stirring the sauces for the cook, that's all. I just tasted them to make sure they were hot enough! Honest, Isabella!"

"That's all right, Porkita. I know what it feels like to be hungry. I was hungry a lot of the time when I was trying to find my way home. Go ahead and taste all you want."

Porkita gave Isabella a wide smile before turning her attention back to the pots of food.

The friendly cook came back and told Isabella she had been granted permission to help them with their project.

"My name is Mary, Your Highness. I will gather the necessary ingredients and then show you how to combine them to make the candies Hogitha loves so much. Then when you are done, I will help you pick a nice basket to put them in."

"Thank you so much! A basket would be perfect!" Isabella replied.

Isabella watched as the cook found what would be needed and placed it on one of the tables. When Mary was finished, Isabella pulled Porkita away from her snacking and led her to the worktable.

"First, we need to mix these ingredients to make the coating for the outside. We'll heat it on the stove and then roll the candied corn through it until it is well coated. Once they have cooled, you can put them in the basket," Mary explained.

"Yum!" added Porkita.

The girls poured the ingredients into the pot as the cook directed. Soon the sauce was complete, and they were ready to coat the candied corn.

"Now, girls, I'll pour a thin layer of the sauce onto this flat board. You should roll the corn pieces through it until they are coated. Then place them over here to cool," instructed the cook. "I'll show you how to do it and then leave you to finish. I need to get back to the preparations for this evening."

Mary picked up a chunk of the candied corn and expertly rolled it through the thick sauce, making sure it was coated on all sides. She set it aside.

"You see, girls, it's easy. Do you have any questions?"

The girls said no and thanked her for all her help. The cook bustled off and the princesses began. They each picked up some candied corn and tried to roll it through the sauce. The sauce was thick and sticky and more ended up on their fingers than on the corn. When they each had finally coated a piece, they set them aside to cool. Isabella picked up a second piece and patiently rolled it. When she turned to set it aside, she was surprised to see the first pieces were missing. Porkita was rolling her second piece.

"Porkita, where are the first pieces we rolled?" Isabella asked.

"Mumph don woah," Porkita answered.

"Porkita! Are you *eating* them?"

Porkita's cheeks turned even pinker than usual as she nodded.

"We're never going to have enough for a gift for Hogitha and Hogden if you eat them all!" Isabella pointed out.

"I'll try not to eat anymore. I promise, Isabella."

By the time Isabella and Porkita had made enough candies to fill a small basket, they were covered in the brown sauce. They had brushed their sticky hands across their faces and had smeary sauce marks on their cheeks and in their hair. Isabella went to the pump to wash her face and hands. When she was finished, she turned to let Porkita use the pump and saw Porkita greedily licking the sauce from her hands. Isabella laughed and shook her head at her friend's appetite. Once Porkita had removed as much as she could with her tongue, she reluctantly washed the rest off at the pump.

"What should we do while we wait for the candies to cool?" asked Isabella.

"Is it lunchtime yet?" asked Porkita, hopefully.

Isabella sighed. "It's a little early. But we can check."

Porkita and Isabella snuck up the servant's staircase to the dining room.

Outside the door, Isabella stopped and laid a hand on Porkita's arm, asking, "What should we tell them we were doing all morning?"

"Let me think. Oh, I know. We can say we were in the Royal Library. Hogitha never goes there, so she won't know that we weren't there."

"Won't they wonder why we're coming in the servant's entrance?" asked Isabella.

"No one should be in there this early. We can be waiting in our chairs when they arrive," answered Porkita.

Loud shouts suddenly came from the dining room. Isabella and Porkita looked at each other in confusion.

"What was that, Porkita?"

"I don't know. I've never heard shouting in the dining room before. Maybe my parents are having a meeting with their advisers."

They put their heads closer to the door and listened.

"Do you think Hogden arrived and he and Hogitha are having a fight?" Porkita asked.

"That could be."

They listened again.

"That doesn't sound like Hogitha, does it, Porkita?"

Porkita shook her head. "No. Can you hear what they are shouting?"

Isabella listened again. This time she could also hear the sound of many heavy boots thudding across the floor, but she couldn't make out any words.

"I can't tell what they are saying, but it sounds like a lot of people are in there. We could open the door just a crack and listen. Then we could see what all the excitement is about."

Porkita hesitated. "But what if it's something we aren't supposed to know about and my parents see us snooping?"

"Well," reasoned Isabella, "no one told us not to come into the dining room at lunchtime, did they? Then we wouldn't be snooping, just coming to have our lunch."

"I'm not sure—"

"Come on, Porkita. Aren't you even a little curious? Maybe it's a surprise for the wedding! Maybe Hogden and his family have arrived and they are having a celebration. I hear boots hitting the floor, so maybe they're dancing. Let's peek in and see."

"Do you think they have tables and tables of food? Maybe even some cakes?"

"Probably. They might even have those sweet pears in thick syrup that you like so much," Isabella tempted.

"Well, we could just peek in and if my sisters are there, then we could join them," Porkita reasoned.

Isabella smiled at her friend and pulled the heavy wooden door open just a crack. The girls saw many figures in black uniforms and black boots. Some were standing in a group talking and some were rushing from place to place.

"That must be Hogden's family," Porkita reasoned. "Do you see my sisters anywhere?"

Isabella searched as much of the room as she could see through the small crack.

"I can't see them, Porkita. Let me open the door a tiny bit more."

As she did, the group broke apart and Isabella gasped loudly. Sitting in chairs with their hands and feet tied was Porkita's whole family.

Chapter Three

Uninvited Guests

Porkita caught sight of them just then and squealed. Isabella let the door shut and put her hand over Porkita's mouth.

"Quiet, Porkita! We can't let them know we're here. Do you know who those soldiers are?"

Porkita shook her head no. Her eyes were wide with fear, and she was pulling relentlessly at Isabella's sleeve without knowing she was doing it.

"I have to open the door again. We have to hear what they are saying to find out why they are here. Don't make any noise, okay?" Porkita nodded.

Isabella opened the door slightly. The royal family was still tied to the chairs and she could see the princesses quietly weeping. She strained to hear what the raised voices were saying. Suddenly, a huge figure in a scarlet uniform strode to the center of the room.

"Well? Where are they?" he barked at a soldier.

"We haven't located them quite yet, Master, but we will have them soon," the soldier answered.

"You idiots!" the imposing figure bellowed, backhanding the soldier and knocking him to the floor. Isabella and Porkita flinched. "Do I not have one capable soldier under my command? How hard can it be to find two young girls? I want Princess Isabella brought to me and I want it done *now!*"

The soldiers scurried to do his bidding. Isabella stepped back and let the door close quietly. Her face was pale as she turned to Porkita.

"They're looking for us!" Isabella whispered frantically. "We have to get out of here right away."

Isabella grabbed Porkita's hand and tried to lead her down the stairs, but Porkita wouldn't budge.

"Porkita! I know you're scared, but we have to go!"

"No!" Porkita answered in a fierce whisper. "I'm not leaving my family. I have to help them." She reached for the door handle.

Isabella stopped her. "Of course we have to help your family, Porkita. I didn't mean we should leave them. But if the soldiers find us, we won't be any help to your family. We have to get out of the palace and go for help!"

Porkita thought for a moment and then nodded. She followed Isabella quietly down the narrow staircase. At the bottom, Isabella stopped to look in both directions. The cooks were still preparing food, unaware of the danger within the palace. Isabella was about to step into the kitchen and warn the servants when she heard heavy boots outside the main doorway. She withdrew to the staircase and felt Porkita's shivering frame pressed against her back. The cooks all looked up from their work as the soldiers burst into the kitchen.

"Everyone in this room is now a prisoner of Rankton the Ruthless. Line up against that wall. Move!"

Isabella saw the frightened cooks obey the soldiers. One of the soldiers walked up and down the line of servants waving a sharp spear in their faces. Isabella saw Mary, the cook who had helped them earlier, and her eyes were darting nervously around the room. Abruptly, Mary spotted Isabella hidden on the stairs. Isabella gestured to Mary to keep quiet and not reveal her presence. The kitchen workers recoiled each time the soldier passed close to them. Isabella thought they were reacting to the weapon he held; then the soldier turned and she saw his face. Even though she was a good distance from him, Isabella shrank away from the sight.

The soldier's face was a mass of green scales that seemed to be constantly expanding and shrinking. His eyes were large blood-red circles with tiny black dots in the center. His two front teeth were huge and hung down almost to his chin. Drool dripped from the end of these teeth; when he spoke, the drool flew in all directions.

"Now," he ordered in a hoarse voice, "one of you is going to tell me where I can find Princess Isabella of Grom and your own Princess Porkita."

No one answered. The repulsive soldier leaned close to one of the cooks and laid the point of his spear against her snout.

"I will ask again," he stated in his raspy voice. "Do you know where the young princesses are?" He pressed the spear harder, and the cook began to weep.

"I-I saw them earlier," Mary blurted out. The soldier removed the spear and turned his attention to Mary. He strode to her side.

"When did you see them?" the soldier demanded.

Mary's voice shook as she answered, "A little while ago. They came in here for a snack."

"Where were they headed next?"

"I think they said they were going up to the third floor ballroom. Yes, they said they were going to play hide and seek up there," Mary lied.

The soldier stared at Mary for a moment, then called to one of his collaborators, "You! Take these slaves up to the dining room to be held with the other captives. The rest of you follow me to the third floor."

Mary chanced one last glance at the doorway where Isabella hid. Isabella gave her a small smile of thanks before Mary was led roughly from the kitchen.

"C'mon!" Isabella grabbed Porkita's hand and led her on tiptoe from the stairway. "We have to get out of the palace without being seen. Do you know a way out?"

"No," answered Porkita. "I think there might be a door at the end of that hallway, but I'm not sure."

"Let's try it," suggested Isabella. They crept across the kitchen slowly, always alert for any sign of the soldiers. They made it to the hallway and then bolted down the short hall toward the only door in sight. Just as they reached the door, they heard the heavy clatter of boots in the kitchen behind them. Isabella grabbed the doorknob and tore the door open. She pushed Porkita through it and followed her, only to slam right into Porkita's back. They weren't outside as they had hoped. They were in a large room filled from ceiling to floor with stored food.

They had stumbled into the palace pantry.

Isabella pulled the door shut behind them and started to search wildly for any way out. Porkita stood staring at the shelves and shelves of food, including one whole wall of shelves filled with ears of corn.

The sound of the soldiers' boots coming down the hall shook Porkita out of her trance. She began helping Isabella look for a way out. As the soldiers came closer, Isabella pulled Porkita behind a row of shelves. Two soldiers burst through the door and glanced quickly around the room. Not seeing the girls, they exited the room and tramped back down the hall. Isabella let out her breath, but froze when she heard a loud crunching in the room with her. She slowly turned her head toward the sound, only to witness Porkita biting into an ear of corn.

"Porkita! How can you eat?" Isabella whispered. "Aren't you afraid?"

"Of course I am!" Porkita responded softly. "And when I'm afraid, I get hungry."

"Forget your stomach for a minute! We have to get out of here."

Porkita dropped what was left of the ear of corn and followed Isabella to the doorway. They opened the door a crack and listened. No sound could be heard. The girls inched their way down the hallway and peeked into the kitchen. It was empty. Choosing the doorway closest to them, they opened it slightly and peered out. It led to the back garden.

The girls slipped out the doorway, looked around to make sure they were alone, and then scampered into the tall rows of corn.

"Do you think anyone saw us?" Porkita asked.

"I don't think so," replied Isabella. As they made their way across the cornfield, she added, "We might be traveling for several days before we find anyone who can help us. Maybe we should pick some of this corn to take with us."

"Where are we going?" asked Porkita. She struggled to carry the ears of corn in her arms until Isabella showed her how to knot the sides of her skirt to form a pouch for carrying. Once the pouch was secure, Porkita quickly filled it with the largest ears she could find.

"I was going to ask you that question. Do you have any neighbors who could help?"

"We have neighbors. Tall, skinny, pale creatures. They aren't close by. We went to their kingdom for a feast once. They didn't seem to like their own cook's meal, because they each only ate one plateful. They looked surprised by how much we enjoyed the food. They never invited us back, though. I don't know how to get there or if they would help."

They reached the end of the first cornfield. Between that field and the next stood a small wooden shack.

"What's in there?" asked Isabella.

"I don't know. Maybe the tools they use to take care of the crops?"

suggested Porkita.

"Let's check inside and see if there is anything we can use."

The girls crept up to the side of the shack and listened. No sound came from within. They snuck to the door and pulled it open a crack. Both girls cried out when they saw the contents of the shack.

There before them stood Mystic. Someone had tied her legs to stakes driven into the ground. A muzzle was strapped to her face and there were scrapes on her legs and body.

"Mystic!" both girls cried as one as they rushed to help their friend. Isabella removed the muzzle while Porkita worked on the ropes binding her legs.

"Thank you," Mystic wheezed, as the muzzle slipped from her face.

"Are you okay? Who did this to you?" Isabella asked.

"A group of soldiers. They grabbed me as I entered the borders of the kingdom," answered Mystic.

"They're all over the palace. They have the royal family tied to chairs in the dining room! They said they were looking for Porkita and me! Who are they?" questioned Isabella.

Mystic stretched her legs now that they were free. She moved to the door of the shed and cautiously checked to see if anyone was nearby.

"We should get out of here. They could come back for me or come here to look for you. Let's move into the far fields. We can hide in there and talk," suggested Mystic.

Carefully, the three friends moved out of the shed and made their way slowly and quietly through the fields until they reached the very edge.

"Tell us what is happening, Mystic," urged Isabella.

"It began about two weeks ago. I had visions of trouble coming to the kingdom. The visions weren't clear at first. They were vague and confusing. But several faces kept appearing. I didn't want to upset the King and Queen until I was absolutely sure, so I left to visit the kingdom of Swinerick about a week ago. One of the faces I saw over and over in my visions was Hogitha's fiancé Hogden. I wanted to talk to him and snoop around his kingdom a little bit. The second face I saw often in my visions was that of his chief adviser, Rankton."

Isabella gasped. "That's the name the soldier used in the kitchen. He told the kitchen workers they were all now prisoners of Rankton the Ruthless!"

"Ruthless is the perfect word to describe him," acknowledged Mystic. Then she continued with her story. "When I arrived at the palace, Hogden behaved normally. He was pleasant and welcoming, inviting me to join him for a meal. We began to talk. He spoke happily about the upcoming wedding and all the feasts that were planned for the soon-to-be-wed couple. I asked him if all had been well in his kingdom lately, and he replied that it had. I then asked him if I might speak to Rankton while I was there and was told that Rankton was away on the business of the kingdom."

"Business of the kingdom, my hoof!" scoffed Porkita.

Mystic ignored the interruption and continued, "I mentioned that I hoped Rankton would be back in time to attend the wedding and was assured that he would be. We spent the evening talking and as it grew late, Hogden invited me to spend the night. I accepted and was offered a room in the palace. I assured Prince Hogden that I would be more comfortable in a nice straw-filled stable, so he quickly ordered one of his guards to show me to their finest stall. I bid him goodnight and followed the guard to the stables. Once he left, I took it upon myself to spend a little time snooping around the grounds and even managed to spend a short time in the palace itself. I found nothing."

"You see," interrupted Porkita again, "Hogden has nothing to do with all of this! He would never do anything to hurt Hogitha!"

Isabella noticed that Mystic didn't agree or disagree with Porkita; she simply resumed her tale. "The few subjects I spoke to felt nothing was amiss and also confirmed that Rankton was away on routine palace business. Satisfied, I went back to my stall and tried to rest. I slept for a short while, but was then awakened by the strongest, clearest vision I have ever had. The vision was filled with greed, danger, betrayal, and deceit. I knew then that I had to return immediately to Sowden and warn the royal family."

Mystic's head drooped as she described what happened next. "I traveled as fast I could, hoping to arrive in time to warn the King, but just as I reached the border, I was stopped by a band of soldiers in black uniforms. They ambushed me and had my mouth muzzled and my legs bound before I could react. How I wish a vision had appeared warning me of their approach!" A noise in the corn caused them all to jump and then freeze. Seconds later, a fat bird flew up from the stalks and they all relaxed.

"What should we do, Mystic?" asked Porkita. "How can we save my family?" Her voice was shaky and tears burned her little round eyes.

"The two of you must leave here," ordered Mystic. "You must travel quickly and secretly and not return until I come to tell you the danger has passed."

"No!" both girls objected.

"You must," repeated Mystic.

"We have to stay here and help you free Porkita's family," argued Isabella. "Unless you know of someone close by we can go to for help?"

Mystic answered, "You can't help me. You can't go to one of the neighboring kingdoms for help. You have to go far away from here and hide in a place where you will be safe."

Porkita began to sob; Isabella put an arm around her shoulders. She continued to argue with Mystic.

"But, Mystic, why can't Porkita and I help? Maybe you could distract the soldiers and Porkita and I could sneak in and untie her family?"

"Isabella, you of all people can't remain here a moment longer. You must leave right away. I will give you directions to a safe place where you and Porkita can stay until I come for you. I promise I will do everything in my power to protect Porkita's family from harm. But you must leave now," insisted Mystic.

"Why are you so insistent that I leave, Mystic? Why won't you let me stay and help?"

"Because, Isabella," answered Mystic in an ominous tone, "the third face that I saw, the face of the being that was in danger, was yours."

Chapter Four

The Bird with Two Faces

Porkita grabbed Isabella's hand in support. Isabella squeezed hard to reassure Porkita. Mystic eyed them both carefully.

"Of course I'm in danger, Mystic," Isabella reasoned. "We're all in danger."

"You don't understand, Isabella," Mystic explained. "Yes, we are all in danger, but in my vision, I saw the evil coming after you in particular. I know that Rankton is evil, and he is trying to find you. I don't know why, and I don't know if Hogden is involved. But I do know that the one who is in the most danger is you. I'm sure of that."

"Why would this Rankton want to find me? I don't even know him!" argued Isabella.

"As I said, I don't know. I only know that you must take Porkita and get far away until it's safe to return," replied Mystic.

Isabella had a sudden thought, "Do you think my parents are okay? Do you think Rankton went to our kingdom first to find me and hurt them in some way?"

"I have to be honest with you, Isabella. I have no idea if your parents are safe. I did not see them as being in danger in my vision. Why aren't they here with you?"

"There was a crisis in our kingdom and they stayed behind for a few days. They are supposed to come before the wedding. What if they come and the soldiers capture them?" asked Isabella.

Mystic answered, "I will help you draw a map that will show you how to reach the village of Teoli. I heard how Lyalus tried to help you reach your home last time. He protected you from the great beast. Lyalus will keep you safe. One of the villagers can travel to Grom and warn your parents not to come to Sowden and ask your father to send his troops here to help. Maybe we can warn your parents before they leave."

"Why can't we go straight to Grom and stop my parents from coming? Why should we go to Teoli first?" questioned Isabella.

"No, Isabella. Stay away from Grom. Rankton will look for you there. Besides, I will feel better if you are with Lyalus. He will guard you with his life. He will do everything he can to make sure you *and* your parents are safe," insisted Mystic.

Porkita agreed, "Listen to Mystic, Isabella. She is wise about these matters. If she says to go to Lyalus, we should go to Lyalus."

Isabella wanted more than anything to go straight to her parents, but she knew Mystic was right. She nodded.

"Good," Mystic said. "Now we need to make a map. Can you find anything we can draw on?"

Isabella and Porkita looked around the cornfield. Porkita grabbed some cornhusks from the ground and held them out to Mystic.

"Will these work?" she asked.

"It would be better if we had something larger," Mystic told her.

"Here," Isabella offered, pulling her skirt up a little, "we can use my slip." Isabella slid her white slip off and laid it on the ground.

"That's fine. Now we need something we can write with," added Mystic. They searched the ground but couldn't find anything useful.

"Wait, I might have something," Porkita cried. She fumbled in the waistband of her skirt and pulled out a red candy stick. "I was saving it for later," she admitted sheepishly.

Isabella tried to draw on the piece of material with the candy, but nothing happened. Porkita took it from her and gave it a good lick.

"Now try," she urged. Isabella did, and it left clear red marks on the slip.

"Look!" Isabella cried. "It's working! Bless your sweet tooth, Porkita!" Porkita blushed and smiled shyly.

Mystic quietly told Isabella the landmarks she needed to draw on the map while Porkita looked out for the soldiers. When Isabella was finished, she pulled her slip back on and set the candy stick on the ground. Porkita picked it up and stuck it back in her waistband.

"For later," she explained.

"Now it's time for us to part ways," Mystic told them. "I think it would be best if you headed through this forest and then up the mountain. The trees will give you cover if the soldiers are searching for you."

"What will you do?" asked Isabella.

"I'm not sure yet," admitted Mystic. "I need to find out exactly what is going on before I can form a plan. But I promise you, I will do everything I can to help your family, Porkita, and I will come to bring the two of you home as soon as possible."

Isabella and Porkita gathered some more corn into their knotted skirts, hugged Mystic, and then cautiously moved into the trees.

The girls moved as swiftly and quietly as they could, interrupted by

Porkita's occasional soft sobs. They were halfway through the forest when Isabella turned and found that Porkita was no longer behind her. Isabella backtracked a short way and found Porkita sitting on the ground quietly crying. Isabella dropped to the ground and put her arms around her.

"Porkita, I know you're scared. I'm scared, too. But we have to keep moving. The soldiers will find us if we don't, and then we won't be able to help your family."

Porkita sniffled and snorted before answering, "I can't go any further, Isabella. My feet hurt, I'm hungry, I'm tired, and I'm so scared! Besides, I know you aren't scared. You aren't scared of anything."

"*Of course* I'm scared, Porkita! I'm scared to death! Why would you think I wasn't scared?"

"Because you're so brave and you tricked the beast to save Lyalus and you found your way home all by yourself and I've never done anything dangerous or daring!" Porkita sobbed.

"Porkita, I was scared from the minute Malachi grabbed me in my throne room until the minute my mother finally recognized me and took me in her arms! And I'm very scared right now. I faced a lot of dangerous, frightening obstacles on my journey, and I survived. But that doesn't mean I wasn't scared. Being brave just means doing what you have to *even though you are scared.*"

"Really?" Porkita asked. "You really are scared, too, Isabella?"

"Of course, Porkita. I'm very scared for us, for your family, for my parents, for Mystic, and for the people of both our kingdoms. Now we can either sit here and cry and quiver until the soldiers find us and take us back to Rankton, or we can get up, find a safe shelter to hide in for the night, and then start out early tomorrow and find help for our families. Which do you want to do?"

Porkita pushed herself up shakily and answered, "Let's go."

They pushed on until the woods were shadowy. Isabella pulled Porkita the last few feet into a narrow opening between two boulders. Once she had Porkita settled, she gathered some branches and spread them on the ground for them to lie on. She collected more branches and pulled them in behind her, hiding the crevice from the view of anyone passing by. Both she and Porkita emptied the corn from their skirts onto the hard floor.

"Try to rest, Porkita," Isabella soothed. "We're going to need all of our strength tomorrow."

Porkita lay down and nibbled halfheartedly on a raw ear of corn.

"Isabella," she murmured.

"What, Porkita?" Isabella asked, nibbling on an ear of corn herself.

"Do you really think we can get help in time to save my family?"

"I don't know, Porkita. All we can do is try. Why don't you eat your candy stick? Maybe it will make you feel better."

"Okay." Then, "Isabella?"

"Yes, Porkita?"

"I wish my family was safe. I wish we were back at the palace eating a huge wedding feast and laughing with my sisters. I wish your parents were there, too, so I could meet them."

"I wish for all that, too, Porkita," Isabella answered sleepily.

"But since I can't have all that," Porkita added, "I'm glad that we're together. There is no one I would rather run away from soldiers with than you, Isabella."

"I'm very glad to be with you too, Porkita. Now, let's get some sleep, okay?"

"Okay, Isabella. Good night."

The girls woke early the next morning and ate some corn for their breakfast. They gathered the leftover corn into their skirts and carefully slipped out the opening. Seeing and hearing nothing alarming, they started moving through the trees again.

The morning passed quickly as they traveled. A group of birds suddenly shot up noisily through the air a short distance in front of them and Isabella caught sight of the sleeve of a soldier's uniform.

"Porkita," she hissed, "they're headed right for us!" She looked around for a hiding place in the woods, but none were readily available.

"Quick, follow me," she whispered. She pulled herself up into the nearest tree, branch by branch. Porkita followed awkwardly. They seated themselves on a sturdy branch quite high in the tree just as the soldiers came into view.

They marched in a long line right below the tree the girls were perched in. Isabella watched their hideous faces until something else caught her eye. Porkita's shoe had slipped partway off and was now dangling from the end of her hoof, poised to drop on the soldiers' heads at any second.

Isabella tugged on Porkita's sleeve and pointed at the hanging shoe. Porkita gasped and leaned out to grab it, but the movement caused the tree branch to groan slightly. Porkita and Isabella froze. The soldiers continued to file past without noticing them. The shoe slipped a bit more. Just as it fell away, Isabella bent forward to grab it, but missed. The shoe dropped into a bush below, and the soldiers stopped. They surrounded the bush and aimed their spears at it. Isabella and Porkita held their breath as one of the repulsive soldiers leaned into the shrub to see what had made the sound. Just then, a rabbit jumped from the bush and the soldiers relaxed and continued on their way.

The princesses waited until the soldiers were far out of sight before climbing down out of the tree.

"That was so close!" said Isabella, sighing. "I thought they would find us for sure when your shoe dropped."

"I know!" exclaimed Porkita. "If that rabbit hadn't jumped out when it did . . ."

"We'd better find your shoe and get out of here."

The girls dug through the bush until they located the shoe and then they were on their way again.

"Isabella?" Porkita huffed, as she struggled to keep up with her friend.

"Yes, Porkita?"

"Where are we headed today? I mean, what did Mystic tell us to look for?"

"She said to pass through these woods and across the meadow. The meadow is where those horrible things hide in the bushes and lure victims in with music. On my last journey, the music put me in some sort of trance. I walked right up to the bushes. Hands with scaly skin and jagged fingernails almost grabbed me. Malachi, disguised as a talking frog, woke me from the trance just in time! But Mystic told me how we can protect ourselves from them. At the edge of the meadow is where the mountain begins. We have to climb the mountain."

"How much farther are we going to go today?" asked Porkita.

Isabella looked at her friend. Porkita's dress was torn, her face had traces of dirt on it and her forehead was covered in perspiration.

"Would you like to stop for a bit and have lunch? If I remember correctly, there is a stream that runs along the edge of the woods. We could have a cool drink and wash our faces. Does that sound good?"

"Oh, yes," Porkita sighed. "Maybe we could find some fruit to eat with our corn."

The two girls found the stream, and it did have berry bushes growing nearby. They washed their faces and drank deeply before picking the bushes clean. Then they sat down and had a lunch of corn and berries.

"Porkita?"

"Mummph?" Porkita answered, her mouth overflowing with food.

"Maybe we should save some of the berries to take with us, in case we can't find anything to eat later."

Porkita looked at the juicy pile of berries, then at Isabella.

"Okay, Isabella. I'll just have a couple more and then we can pack the rest," answered Porkita, as she reached for another large handful of berries. Isabella smiled and finished eating an ear of corn.

When the girls were through with their meal, Isabella showed Porkita how to make a container to hold water. They filled the containers and Porkita headed toward the meadow.

"Porkita, wait!" Isabella called. When Porkita stopped, Isabella told her, "Take off your slip and tie it around your head so your ears are covered."

"Isabella, what are you talking about?"

"If we can't hear the music coming from the bushes, it can't put us into a trance," Isabella explained.

Both girls slid their slips off and tied them tightly around their heads. Then they looked at each other, clasped hands and ran as fast as they could across the meadow. They did not stop until they were safely through the meadow and into the forest at the lower half of the mountain. Both girls doubled over, trying to catch their breath, and Porkita was drenched in sweat. Isabella took the slip off her head and gestured to Porkita to do the same. They pulled the slips back on under their dresses and then slowly headed into the woods.

The sun dropped low in the sky and still they continued. Finally at dusk they reached the part of the mountain where the woods ended and the rocky slope began.

"I think we should stop for the night," Isabella said. "Once we leave these woods, there is nothing but rocks and dirt for a long time. I came over this mountain when I happened upon your palace last time. It would be foolish to try to climb the top part of the mountain in the dark."

Porkita dropped to the ground, exhausted.

"Wait, Porkita!" Isabella cried, pulling her back to her feet. "We have to search for a place where the soldiers can't find us if they pass through here."

"I can help you," squeaked a voice from above.

Porkita squealed in fear, and Isabella's voice trembled as she asked, "Who said that?"

"Me. Up here. I said that," answered the voice.

Porkita and Isabella looked up and saw a strange-looking bird perched on the limb of a tree. The bird was squat and fat and had dirty brown feathers. But the strangest part was its face. One side was brown with a beady black eye, while the other side was deep red with a large yellow eye. The left side of the beak was orange and the right side was black. The brown side was flat and matted while the red side was bright and fluffy. It was as though the bird had two separate faces.

"Who are you?" asked Isabella.

"My name is Yokum," replied the bird.

"It's nice to meet you, Yokum. How can you help us?" Isabella asked.

"I can tell you where there is a safe place to spend the night," answered Yokum.

"That would be very helpful to us, Yokum. Thank you," said Isabella.

The bird turned its head so only the red side was showing and said, "If you go through that group of trees right there and around the big boulder, you will find a cave where no soldiers will bother you."

"Thank you, Yokum," Isabella called as she and Porkita headed toward the cave.

"Wait!" the bird called and when they looked back, only the ugly brown side of his face was showing. "Don't go into the cave," he cried. "There are animals that sleep in there, and they aren't friendly if you wake them up."

"Then where can we go?" asked Porkita.

The red side showed itself again and spoke, "You could sleep in that big nest over there. It is high off the ground and you will be safe."

"That's a good idea. Thank you," Isabella said again.

They had only taken two steps when the brown side spoke, "The giant bird that lives in that nest won't be very happy when she finds you. You should make a nest of your own in those bushes over there."

"I disagree," squawked the red side.

"You would probably send them into that hole," countered the brown side.

"I would not. But that hole is cozy and warm."

"And that's why all the snakes that live there love it so much," replied the brown side.

"Well, there are animals with sharp teeth in the bushes you wanted to send them into," insisted the red side.

"You know that's not true. Those bushes are safe," responded the brown side.

Porkita and Isabella stood for a few more minutes watching the bird fight with itself. Then they shook their heads and walked quietly away. They found a glade with a trickling stream and used branches to build a little shelter near its edge. Carefully, they crawled inside and quickly fell asleep.

When they crawled out after a breakfast of corn, the two-faced bird greeted them immediately.

"Good morning, ladies!" the brown side chirped.

"It's not that great of a morning," grumbled the red side.

"Good morning, Yokum," called Isabella. "It's nice to see you again, but we have to be on our way."

"Which way are you going today?" asked the brown side.

"We are heading over the top of the mountain," replied Porkita.

"Make sure you stay to the left," advised the red side, "the climbing is much easier on that side."

"I would stay to the right," advised the brown side. "There aren't as many large boulders on that path."

"The left!"

"The right!"

Isabella looked at Porkita and rolled her eyes. "Uh, we'll take your advice, Yokum. Thank you for everything." The girls gathered up their things and made their way out of the woods.

"Which way are we going to go?" asked Porkita.

"I'm not sure, but I think the brown side of his face tells the truth and the red side tries to confuse us," answered Isabella. "So let's stay to the right and see what happens."

They started climbing the rocky part of the mountain, careful to stay to the right. They hadn't gone far when they heard a familiar voice.

"Hello again, little girls!" It was Yokum.

"Hello, Yokum," Isabella called. "Sorry, we can't talk right now. We need to concentrate on reaching the top." She was anxious to be rid of the strange bird.

"You'll never reach it if you go this way," screeched the red side of the face. "There are too many obstacles. You really should go to the left."

"Don't listen. He is trying to lead you into danger. Keep going this way and you'll be fine," the brown side assured them.

"Left!"

"Right!"

"Left!"

"Right!"

"Thanks again, Yokum. You'd better get back into the woods now," hinted Isabella.

The bird screeched once more and then retreated into the woods.

"Does that bird ever tell the truth?" asked Porkita, as they made their way higher.

"I don't know, but his screeching was making my head hurt!"

The girls found the rocks getting larger and more difficult to scale as they climbed. Soon they reached a point where they could no longer make it over the boulders.

"What do we do now, Isabella?" asked Porkita.

"I guess we have to go back down a little way and then go to the left. I thought the brown side of the bird was telling the truth, didn't you? Now I don't know what to believe."

They climbed back down until the boulders leveled out, then made their way to the left. They found a spot where the rocks were manageable and slowly made their way to the top. The girls collapsed on the ground, panting.

"I told you to go to the left," squeaked Yokum, reappearing.

"You also told us to go to the right," complained Isabella, angrily.

"I didn't tell you to go to the right," the red side argued.

"You should have listened," the brown side told them.

"Now, if you want to find the best way down the other side—" started the red side.

"No more advice! You say something different every time you talk! We don't believe anything you say!" hollered Porkita.

Yokum stared at the girls for a moment and then flew away.

"I think I hurt his feelings," admitted Porkita, "but he was so confusing. I never knew if he was telling the truth! And I get grumpy when I'm hungry, and I'm so hungry!"

"Don't worry about it, Porkita. Now that we are at the top, let's have a snack and look around. There is something I hope to see from here."

Porkita crunched on corn as they looked down the other side. After a moment, Isabella cried out.

"There! Do you see it? That house surrounded by trees? That's Grammy's house! Grammy will help us!"

"Grammy is the old woman you met on your first journey, isn't she?" asked Porkita. "The one who took you in and made clothes and supplies for you?"

"Yes. You'll love her. She's so nice, and she makes the best muffins you have ever tasted! She has a pet bird named Orion, and he's magnificent! I don't always understand all the words Grammy uses, but I can usually figure out what she means. Some of her words are so funny! Oh, let's hurry, Porkita!"

"Here, Isabella. We can lower ourselves down right here if we use these holes to put our hands and feet in," cried Porkita excitedly.

"No!" shuddered Isabella. "There are furry little creatures living in those holes! I found them when I climbed up here last time. I almost fell because they were biting my hands and feet. We'll have to go farther to the left and see if we can find an easier way to get down."

Isabella and Porkita made their way to the left and found a spot where they could lower themselves down without putting their hands in any holes. Before long, they were past the rocky part of the mountain and into the forest.

"Isabella," said Porkita, "I know you're in hurry to reach Grammy's house, but it has been an awful long time since breakfast, and I only had that one ear of corn since then."

"I'm sorry, Porkita," Isabella responded, stopping. "I was in such a hurry to see Grammy; I forgot we hadn't eaten lunch. Let's stop in this glen and have a nice rest."

The princesses sat on the ground and took out the corn and berries they had saved. They only had four pieces of corn and a handful of berries left since some had fallen from their skirts while they were climbing. Porkita wanted to go back and find the scattered food, but Isabella convinced her that they would have plenty to eat once they reached Grammy's house.

As they rested, an animal jumped from the bushes. It reminded Isabella of the cats that roamed the gardens at the palace, only this creature was much bigger and definitely not as friendly. He circled the princesses with his thick tail swishing and his sharp teeth bared. The girls huddled together, Porkita squealing and Isabella looking for something to use as a weapon. The cat growled and howled as it moved even closer. When it snapped its teeth at Porkita's arm, she screamed in fear.

"A-a-a-a-h-h-h-h-h!" In swooped Yokum, squawking at full volume, claws outstretched as they grazed the cat's head.

"You don't want to eat these girls!" he screeched. "They're not at all tasty!"

"You'll find much sweeter girls farther up the mountain!" the red side offered loudly.

"No, the sweeter girls are down the mountain!" hollered the brown side.

The whole time Yokum was hollering, he was flying in circles around the cat's head, just out of reach.

"These girls are sour and will make your stomach ache!" insisted the red side.

"No," argued the brown side, "They will make your head ache because they are too sweet!"

"Sour!" bawled the red side.

"Sweet!" screamed the brown side.

"Stomach!" roared the red side.

"I say head!" yelled the brown side.

"Sour! Stomach!"

"Sweet! Head!"

The wild cat was slinking further and further away from the flapping, raucous bird and finally turned tail and ran into the woods.

"Oh, thank you, Yokum!" Isabella cried. "You've saved our lives for sure!"

"And I was so mean to you!" Porkita apologized. "Thank you, Yokum, for chasing that horrible creature away!"

"It was my idea to help you," bragged the brown side.

"It was not!" insisted the red side. "It was completely my idea."

"I had the idea, and I came up with a plan!" the red side squawked.

"You always take credit for everything I do!" screeched the brown side, as the ugly bird flew lopsidedly away.

Chapter Five

Target Practice

Isabella and Porkita hurried through the woods on the bottom half of the mountain. The air was sweet and cool and made the trek easier. Even though they moved quickly, it was evening by the time they stumbled through the last of the trees and saw Grammy's cabin standing in the valley.

"I don't see any light, Isabella. Do you think anyone is there?"

"Grammy is probably sleeping, but she won't mind being woken up when she sees that it's me. Let's go; the door is around this way."

The girls walked onto the front porch and knocked on the door. There was no answer.

Isabella called out, "Grammy! It's me, Isabella!"

There was still no answer. Isabella pushed open the door and walked into the cabin. Everything looked normal. There were still pretty hand-stitched quilts and pillows everywhere. The room smelled like spices and wood-smoke. Orion's cage stood where it had been when Isabella was there last, its door hanging open.

"Where do you think she is?" asked Porkita.

"I don't know. She's pretty old, and she told me she doesn't travel much anymore. Wherever she is, she probably took Orion with her."

Just then, there was a great flapping sound as the majestic bird flew in the door and landed on Isabella's shoulder.

"Orion! You're here! Hello, pretty bird," Isabella cooed as she stroked the bird's feathers. "Where is Grammy, Orion?"

The bird gave Isabella a quick nuzzle and then flew out the door. Isabella and Porkita followed. The bird glided toward the fruit orchards. The girls followed him until he dove down and landed on a branch in a massive apple tree.

"Orion, where is Grammy? I need to find Grammy!"

"Isabella," a soft voice called. "Is that you, girl?"

Isabella walked around to the other side of the large tree and found the old woman seated on the ground with her back against the trunk.

Isabella quickly dropped to the ground beside her. "Grammy! Are you all right? Are you hurt? What are you doing out here?"

Grammy took Isabella's hand. "I'm fine, child. I'm so glad to see you! Have you been wanderin' around all this time looking for yer home?"

"No, Grammy. I found my home, but now I'm in trouble again. I'll tell you all about it, but first let me help you into the house." Isabella started to lift Grammy from the ground, but Grammy stopped her.

"Wait, Isabella! We can't go to the house! Some soldiers have been here, asking pertang questions about ya! Horrible, hideous soldiers! They wanted to know if I had seen Princess Isabella of Grom. Described ya to a tee. I knowed right away they was quesels! Told them you headed off in that direction." Grammy pointed away from the mountain. "Said they'd be back, so's Orion and I've bin hiding out here in the orchard. If'n we go to the house, they might find us."

"When were they here, Grammy?"

"One lighttime ago, darlin'. Orion and me were jest sittin' down to evening meal when they burst thru the door. Ugly critters, they were. Shoutin' and threatenin' me somethin' fierce. Waving spears all over the place!"

Porkita stepped out of the dark and into Grammy's view.

"Well now, who do we have here?" asked Grammy.

"Grammy, this is my best friend, Princess Porkita of Sowden. Porkita, this is Grammy."

"Lan' sakes! Another princess! Well, well, the soldiers said you was travelin' with another girl, but they didn't say she was royalty! Mighty pleasin' to meet another friend of Isabella's, Your Highness."

"Just call me Porkita. And I feel as though I already know you from everything Isabella has told me! May I call you Grammy?"

"Course you can, honey! I knowed if'n you were Isabella's best friend, you'd have to be someone special. And aren't you a bowjuse thing!"

Porkita looked at Isabella in confusion. Isabella shrugged her shoulders and smiled, so Porkita smiled and thanked Grammy.

"What them soldiers looking fer you fer, Isabella?" Grammy asked.

"I don't know, Grammy," Isabella answered. "I was visiting Porkita when they broke in the palace and took Porkita's family captive. We overheard them talking, so we knew they were looking for us. We escaped, and now we are trying to get word to my father to send help. We were hoping you would be able to help us."

"Let me think a bit," Grammy responded. "If you two can hide out here for a piece, I could rustle up some gnawback fer ya and a sleep-throw or two, then sneak em out to ya. How'd that be?"

"That sounds wonderful, Grammy! But will it put you in danger?" worried Isabella.

"Nah! Don't worry, child. If those soldiers come back, Orion and I will take care of em. I'll tell em I'm packin' up to go on a trip. If they don't believe me, I'll give em a good crack on their nod, I will!" replied Grammy fiercely.

"I don't want to cause you any trouble, Grammy," Isabella said. "Maybe you should stay here in hiding and Porkita and I should just leave right away. It might be safer for you if we did."

"You sit down and gnaw on some of this fruit, girls, and I'll be back quicker than a lofert in a grease pit. Come on, Orion, we got work ta do!" Grammy hoisted herself off the ground and moved away rather swiftly for a woman of her years.

"Isabella, what's a lofert? And what does gnaw mean? I couldn't understand her at all!"

"I don't understand a lot of her words either, but the important thing is she's all right. I was worried when we didn't find her in the cabin. I think she said to help ourselves to some fruit from these trees, and she's packing some more food for us to take with us and maybe a blanket or two," explained Isabella.

"Yum!" exclaimed Porkita. "Let's not waste time. Let's pick some fruit."

68

The two girls filled their knotted skirts with ripe apples and pears and then sat down to sample a few.

"Why do you think those awful soldiers are looking for us?" Porkita asked as she crunched into a juicy apple.

"I wish I knew, Porkita. If we only knew what they wanted, we could give it to them and maybe they would leave our families alone."

"If they just wanted gold or riches, they wouldn't need to have you and me, right? They could just take it and leave," reasoned Porkita, apple juice dripping from her chin.

"I don't think they are just looking for riches. I think they want something more important. I just don't know what it is," said Isabella.

The girls sat silent for a while, each lost in her own thoughts of family and home. When they heard someone approaching in the darkness, they scrambled behind the large tree.

"No fear, girls; it's jest ole Grammy. I brought some goodies fer ya."

Grammy was dragging a large sack behind her. She held it open to show the girls its contents.

"I put in some vegetables from my patch, some muffins I baked afore the soldiers come, two sleep-throws, and a few other things I thought yer could use."

Isabella saw the quilts Grammy had included and threw her arms around the old woman's neck.

"Thank you so much, Grammy! You don't know how much this means to us! You didn't see any sign of trouble while you were in there, did you?"

"Nah! I think those varmin are far from here by now. You girls can sleep in the cabin or bunk down here in the orchard if'n you want."

"I love you, Grammy, and I would love to spend some time with you, but I think we should get away from here in case the soldiers come back," explained Isabella.

"But Isabella," Porkita complained, a touch of tired whine in her voice, "the soldiers are nowhere near here, and she has an actual bed we can sleep in!"

"But Porkita, the soldiers might come back! We can't let them find us, and we can't put Grammy and Orion in any more danger. We have to leave here right away."

Porkita nodded reluctantly, and the two girls hugged Grammy goodbye. Grammy warned them to be careful and told them to come back to visit as soon as they could. Orion flew with them for a short distance until Isabella urged him to go back and watch over Grammy.

It wasn't very long before both girls were forced to give into exhaustion. They dragged their bag of supplies into some heavy brush, pulled the quilts over themselves, and slept.

The sun was high in the sky by the time the girls woke up. They ate a quick breakfast and dug through the bag Grammy had packed. It had been too dark last night to see all that she had given them. Besides the quilts and food, Grammy had packed two jugs full of water, a knife, a pot, a comb, and some homemade soap that smelled like flowers. She also added two robes that Isabella and Porkita assumed were Grammy's old ones, since they were so large. Isabella swam in hers, while the one Porkita tried on was long for her but not that big around the middle.

"These will be nice to slip on when we want to wash our dresses," said Isabella.

"I've never seen material quite like this," commented Porkita, running the rough fabric between her fingers.

"It isn't as soft as the cloth our dresses are made of, but it doesn't tear as easily," Isabella told her. "Grammy made me two dresses from this kind of material the last time I was here, and they held up throughout my travels. I'll bet we'll be glad we have these before our journey is over."

Porkita helped Isabella stuff all their supplies into the cloth bag, except the two jugs of water which Porkita carried in her knotted skirt.

"Which way are we headed today?"

Isabella pulled up her skirt and consulted the map.

"Mystic said that once we came down off the mountain, we should head in that direction until we reach a big swamp," Isabella replied, pointing to the east.

"All right then. Let's go."

The two traveled across an open field and through a small wooded area before reaching the enormous swamp. They stopped at its edge.

"It would have been pretty hard for us to have missed this!" Isabella cried out. "It's huge!" She checked her map again. "On my first trip, I crossed a swamp and sank in mud up to my chest. If Phinius hadn't come along and pulled me out, I would have died there. Mystic said there isn't any shifting sand in this swamp, but she told me we should go around the right edge to be safe. Are you ready?"

"Isabella, that doesn't make any sense! It will take much longer to go all the way around the edge! If there isn't any sand to sink in, I think we should go straight through the middle. We shouldn't waste any more time," Porkita argued.

"I know it would be quicker to go straight across, Porkita, but we should listen to Mystic. She has been through here, and if she says to stay along the edge, we should stay along the edge."

"Isabella," replied Porkita, impatiently, "I am tired, my feet hurt, and I am worried about my family. I am also hungry for corn pudding, corn casserole, and cakes and pies and—"

"I understand, Porkita, but—"

"Well, I think it is silly to waste time going around the edge and *I* am

72

going through the center. I will wait for you on the other side. I'm going to sit and rest my feet and pretend the fruit I eat is actually creamed corn cake." And with that, she stormed off into the swamp.

"Porkita, no! Wait! You don't know what might be in there!"

Isabella rushed to catch up with Porkita, but Porkita was in a huff and moving quickly. As she followed, Isabella felt something sting her cheek. She reached up to touch it and felt something slimy. Then her fingers started to sting. Greenish-yellow goo dripped from them. Before she could figure out where it had come from, she heard Porkita scream.

Isabella darted forward and saw Porkita holding a hand to her forehead.

"Porkita, what happened?"

"I don't know," she cried, "Something hit my forehead and it hurts!" Tears were streaming down her face. Isabella moved Porkita's hand and saw the same green slime that had been on her own cheek. She quickly looked around to see where the slime was coming from, but all she saw was a fat blue bullfrog sitting on a log. As she watched him, he puffed up his cheeks and a stream of green goo shot straight toward Isabella's face. Isabella dropped to the ground, pulling Porkita with her.

"Porkita, we have to get out of here! That big frog over there is spitting something at us! That's what hit you. Stay down and crawl."

The two girls crawled a few feet forward with Isabella leading the way. Isabella looked over her shoulder to make sure the frog hadn't followed. When she turned back, a big blue bullfrog was perched on the ground inches from her face, its cheeks puffed and ready.

"Roll, Porkita!" she screamed, as she threw herself and the supply bag to the left. The stinging spit just missed her, but Porkita didn't react fast enough. It hit her full in the cheek, and she screamed again.

Isabella had rolled into a marshy spot and now she and the bag were soaked. She stumbled to her feet, her wet dress plastered to her legs and screamed, "Run, Porkita!!"

She grabbed Porkita's hand and pulled her to her feet. The two girls sprinted forward through the knee-deep water, pushing reeds aside as they ran. They pushed through a tall patch of swamp-grass to find three more bullfrogs perched on a log, just waiting for them.

"No-o-o-o!" screeched Porkita. Isabella grabbed her hand again and veered to the right. Another bullfrog waited on a lily pad. Porkita was hysterical and barely able to run. Isabella kicked at the frog just as it puffed its cheeks. It fell off the lily pad and the girls rushed past it. Hurdling over logs and splashing through pools of stagnant water, Isabella dragged Porkita to the swamp's edge. She saw the fat bullfrogs waiting in every direction, circling, surrounding them, but she pushed on. Twice more she felt stinging pain, once on her arm and once on her neck, but she didn't stop until they were out of the swamp and into the woods.

Isabella dropped to the ground, panting, and pulled Porkita down next to her. Porkita's eyes and mouth were wide open, frozen in an expression of horror.

"It's all right now, Porkita," Isabella soothed. "We're out of there. They can't hurt you anymore." She ripped off a piece of her wet skirt, poured clean water from the jug on to it and wiped the slime from Porkita's face. Underneath the slime were bright red welts with small bubbly blisters on them.

"Wait here a minute, Porkita. I want to try and find a plant Phinius showed me that might ease the stinging. It grows in wooded areas, so there might be some here." Isabella searched the ground until she found what she was looking for. She broke open the swollen leaf and applied some of the musky-scented gel to Porkita's sores. Porkita had still not spoken a word. She just sat staring straight ahead with that horrified look on her face. Isabella applied the gel to her own burns and then took out one of Grammy's quilts and wrapped it around Porkita's shoulders. She pulled Porkita to her feet and led her slowly deeper into the woods.

"Let's get away from that nasty swamp," she urged Porkita. "Let's find a nice grove with a sparkling pool of water where we can stop for the night. We'll have a nice dinner. Maybe build a fire and cook some of Grammy's vegetables. Would you like that, Porkita?" But there was still no response. Isabella kept talking in a gentle voice until she found the perfect spot. There was a tiny pool of water, fed by a pretty little waterfall. The water tumbled peacefully off several large rocks and made a comforting sound.

Isabella guided Porkita to the ground and then proceeded to set up camp. She first built a circle of stones and in it lit a small fire. She then used the knife to chop up fresh vegetables. She placed these in the pot with some water and set it on the fire. Isabella dragged a log over next to the fire and seated Porkita on it. When the vegetables had cooked, she took them out of the pot and placed them on a piece of bark to cool. While they were cooling, she chopped up pieces of apple, put them in the pot with some water and set it on the fire.

Isabella picked up the vegetables and using a small flat stick as a scoop, she tried to feed some to Porkita. She managed to persuade Porkita to eat several spoonfuls and then ate some herself. When the fruit was stewed, she shared that with Porkita also. Isabella laid her quilt on the ground a short distance from the fire and helped Porkita lie down on it. She pulled Porkita's quilt over top and murmured comforting words to Porkita until she felt her friend's body relax into sleep. Only then did she allow herself to rest.

When Isabella woke up the next morning, she heard whimpering sounds. She sat up to find Porkita hunched by the fire-ring. Her shoulders were shaking and she was making pitiful sounds. Isabella jumped up and went to her friend.

"Porkita, are you all right?" she asked.

"Oh, Isabella," Porkita sobbed, throwing herself into Isabella's arms, "It was *so* awful! All those horrid frogs and that disgusting stuff they were shooting at us! They were everywhere! I was so afraid and it burned so bad!"

"I know, Porkita. It was awful! But it's over now, and we're okay. The sores don't hurt nearly as much today, do they?" Porkita shook her head. "They will probably be totally gone by tomorrow. We're safe and together and we're going to be just fine."

"You took care of me, Isabella. You dragged me out of the swamp and saved me from those horrible things. I will never forget it, Isabella. You are the best friend anyone could ever have." Porkita's voice caught in her throat.

"We saved each other, Porkita. And you are the best friend I could ever have." She gave her a tight squeeze. "Now, I'm going to fix some breakfast for my very best friend," she announced in a cheerful voice, "and after we eat, we are going to get moving so we can save our families! Right?"

Porkita nodded her head and tried to sound as cheerful. "That's right! I'm going to help my best friend make breakfast. Suddenly, I'm starving! What do you want me to do?"

The girls worked together to start the fire and cook some more fruit. Isabella thought hot food would brighten Porkita's spirits. It seemed to work, judging by the amount she ate. Porkita was happily licking her bark dish clean while Isabella rinsed out the cooking pot.

"That was delicious, Isabella! How did you learn to cook so well?"

"On my last journey, I watched Malachi, Phinius, the tribes-people, and Grammy, so I learned a few things. Of course, watching Malachi cook taught me what not to do! He was a rotten cook! He could take delicious ingredients, put them together in a pot, and somehow make the whole thing come out disgusting. Grammy could put the exact same ingredients in a pot and make them come out wonderful! I could never understand that."

"Well," stated Porkita, "I would say there is only one thing wrong with your cooking."

"What's that?"

"You didn't make enough!" Porkita teased, as she gave her dish one last lick.

The two friends packed up their belongings and consulted Mystic's map. It was faded from the swamp water, but there was still enough pink traces to show them the way.

"Mystic said we should cross this field and find a giant boulder shaped like a fist on the other side. That's our next landmark," Isabella informed her.

"Then let's get going!" Porkita shouted, starting out of the campsite.

"Porkita, wait! I want to talk to you about something."

"What is it, Isabella?"

"There are a lot of dangerous things outside our palace walls, things we've never heard of or seen. We have to follow Mystic's map exactly, or we could get in serious trouble. And neither one of us can wander off by herself. We have to do this together, okay?"

"It's okay, Isabella, I know what you're trying to tell me. I learned my lesson last night. I am going to stick to your side like glue. You won't be able to get rid of me!" With that, Porkita turned and walked out of the grove.

Isabella shook her head, sighed, and picked up the pack. She threw it over her shoulder and hurried to catch up to her companion.

Chapter Six

Sticks and Stones

It took most of the morning to cross the field. By the time they found the boulder shaped like a fist, they were tired, thirsty, and slightly sunburned. They sat for a moment to rest, take a drink of the now-warm water, and eat a piece of fruit for energy.

"Isabella, I am exhausted. My shoes are killing my feet. I'm not used to walking so much. I don't think these shoes were made for walking, anyway. I think they were just made to match my dress. We have been traveling for days, and we aren't even halfway through Mystic's map! I think we should just stay here and wait for someone to find us," Porkita suggested crossly.

"What if the soldiers are the ones who find us? We can't give up now, Porkita! Our families are depending on us! We have to go on even if we are tired. I know we can do it! Let's just cross this boulder field, and then we'll stop for a nice long rest. Maybe we should try to walk more at night. The soldiers wouldn't be able to see us in the dark and it wouldn't be so hot! Then we could find a nice shelter to sleep in during the day. What do you think?"

"Traveling in the dark?" Porkita swallowed hard. "With all the creatures roaming about? I think I would rather bake under the afternoon sun than do that, thank you."

Isabella shrugged. "Okay. It was just an idea. We'll keep traveling in the daylight then. Let's go."

The girls gathered up their supplies and started into the boulder field. The field seemed to stretch out endlessly before them. It was hard work climbing over each boulder, made harder by the hot sun beating down on them.

"Isabella!" Porkita whispered. "I think---I think that boulder over there just moved."

"Porkita," Isabella replied, wiping sweat from her brow and starting over the next large rock, "It's a rock. It can't move. You're just tired and hot."

At that instant, the boulder Isabella was perched on lifted off the ground and started moving forward.

"Porkita!" Isabella screamed. "Help me!"

"I can't!" Porkita screamed back. "Mine's moving, too!"

Isabella looked back to find Porkita holding on to a large boulder for dear life as it moved jerkily across the ground.

"What should we do?" hollered Porkita.

"I don't know!" shouted Isabella. "If we try to jump off, we'll hit the other rocks and get hurt!"

"So what do we do?" Hysteria tinged her voice.

"Hang on!" Isabella yelled, as the rock she rode climbed over another rock.

Isabella held on while her boulder ambled over three more rocks. When it bumped up against a rock twice its size and stopped, she scrambled off. She saw Porkita clinging to her rock. Porkita's rock stopped and Isabella yelled to her to climb off. She did, but the next rock she climbed on started moving, too.

"Isabella!" she yelled. "It's happening again!"

"Don't worry, Porkita! I'm right behind you." Isabella jumped on a rock and waited for it to take off in Porkita's direction, but it remained still. She scrambled to the next rock. It, too, remained still. She decided to catch up with Porkita on her own. She stood up on her rock and jumped to the next rock. As her feet hit it, it lifted up and started to move forward. She quickly straddled the rock and held on. Her boulder was heading in the same direction as Porkita's. Twice more the boulder she was riding on stopped, and she had to transfer to another one. Finally, she caught up to Porkita.

Porkita had her eyes shut tight as she repeated, "I'll be all right, I'll be all right, I'll be all right," over and over.

"I'm here now, Porkita. We're almost through the field. Just hang on a few minutes more."

The boulders took them almost to the edge. When they stopped, Isabella and Porkita hopped off and then turned back to get a better look at the moving rocks.

"Why, I don't think they are rocks, Porkita!" Isabella exclaimed. "Look at that one standing up right there! It has legs and feet!" She bent down and put her face close to one of the rocks that had carried her. "Look, Porkita! It has a face!"

That's when the rock lifted up and sank its hard teeth into Isabella's arm. She screamed as Porkita grabbed her and pulled her out of the field. Isabella began sobbing as throbbing pain engulfed her arm.

"Let me see." Porkita gently pushed Isabella's sleeve up to reveal big teeth marks that were already darkening into a bruise. Porkita took one look at the wound and wheeled around to face the rock field.

"You big, stupid rocks!" she bellowed. "Look what you did to my friend! She is the nicest person I know and you hurt her!" Isabella stared, her mouth hanging open. She had never seen this startling side of Porkita. She forgot about the pain in her arm as she watched Porkita's ferocious display.

"You are nothing but a bunch of stupid, stupid rocks with legs and faces and stuff! I should break you in pieces! Little pieces of stupid rock! Tons of—"

Dozens of "rocks" across the field abruptly reared up on their back legs and growled. Porkita stumbled back a few steps and then pulled Isabella to her feet.

"I think they got the message. Let's get moving," Porkita urged, as she dragged Isabella quickly away by her uninjured arm. They hadn't gone more than twenty feet when Isabella stumbled. She dropped to her knees and began making squeaking sounds. Porkita dropped down beside her.

"Isabella, it's okay! We're safe! Is it your arm? Does it hurt terribly?" Isabella nodded, but didn't look up. "What can I do? Is there a plant I can pick that will help? You have to stop crying long enough to answer me, or I can't help you! I don't know what to do! Isabella, please!"

Isabella raised her head and looked straight at Porkita. Tears were streaming down Isabella's face and her shoulders were shaking violently.

"You---you---were so---funny," she gasped, laughter overtaking her once more. "Yelling at---those---rocks! Th-th-threatening to smash them to bits!"

Porkita sputtered, "Y-y-you were *laughing*! I was worried sick about you, and you were *laughing*! Of all the---I tried to help and--- what were you--- I should leave you here to rot!" With that she started pacing back and forth. "I thought you were in terrible pain! I thought you were crying hysterically! And you were *laughing* at me! At *me*!"

Isabella tried to contain her laughter, but couldn't. "I'm s-s-sorry, P-P-orkita. I really am! But if you could have seen yourself! You were so angry, I almost felt sorry for the rocks. Shaking your fist and telling them you were going to---going to pound them into pieces!" Isabella rocked backwards with laughter.

Porkita glared at her for another moment and then smiled. Soon the smile became a giggle, then a laugh. Then she was on the ground next to Isabella squealing and snorting helplessly.

When their laughter had finally subsided, Porkita asked, "What are we going to do about your arm?"

"It's not too bad right now. The teeth didn't break through the skin;

they just bruised it. If we could find a stream, I could put some cold mud on it. That's supposed to help."

"Why didn't Mystic tell us about the moving rocks?" wondered Porkita.

"I'm not sure. Maybe she forgot, or maybe they never moved when she went through the field. She kind of flies across the ground, so maybe she didn't realize they were able to move," reasoned Isabella.

"What do we have to look for now?"

"Let me check." She lifted her skirt and looked at the map on her slip. "See, there's the rock shaped like a fist, and after that, we head straight forward until we reach a river and then follow that for a long way." Isabella dropped her skirt and turned to Porkita. "I know you're tired, but it doesn't look like it's too far to the river. We could probably reach it by dark. Then I could make a mudpack for my arm, and we could camp for the night. I don't want to stay here in case those rocks can walk this far. Does that sound okay to you?"

"All right, as long as I can have something to eat while we walk. I'm hungry again!"

Isabella pulled a couple of pieces of fruit from the pack and tossed them to Porkita. She munched them happily as they continued. The girls followed the map until they reached the river. It was wide and flowing rapidly. It reminded Isabella of the river she had to cross when she first escaped from Malachi. One of the stones she jumped on to cross that river had actually been a reptile that almost bit her.

They found a small area by the river that was sheltered by leafy trees. Isabella worked on making a mudpack for her arm while Porkita gathered branches for a fire. Isabella showed Porkita how to start a fire the way Malachi had taught her. At first, nothing happened and Porkita grew frustrated. But when she managed to produce a spark and then a flame, she was thrilled.

"Isabella! I did it! I started a fire!" she cried.

"I know. I was so excited the first time I did it, too. It's great to be able to do things for yourself, isn't it?"

Isabella showed Porkita how to cut up the vegetables and cook them in the pot over the fire. Porkita grew more excited with each new accomplishment.

"Oh, Isabella," she sighed, as she took the first bite of the food, "this tastes so good! I can't believe we cooked this!" She finished her portion and then scraped the pot clean.

The girls lay in their quilts after dinner, giggling and talking until they drifted off to sleep.

By morning, the swelling on Isabella's arm had gone down, and it wasn't nearly as sore, although it was still deeply bruised. After breakfast, Isabella and Porkita packed up their supplies and began to follow the curve of the river. The terrain was flat, so they were able to cover a large distance quickly.

When they stopped for a lunch of fruit and muffins, Porkita asked, "What do we look for now? What's next on Mystic's map?"

Isabella checked her slip and replied, "We have to follow the river until we see two huge trees bent together to form a giant arch. I think we still have quite a long way to go before we reach it. Maybe by dark." Isabella stretched the slip out and checked the rest of the map.

"Look, Porkita!" she exclaimed, pointing to the map. "After the arch, we have to cross a field, go through a forest, and then over a hill and we will be at Lyalus's village! We're almost there! If we hurry, maybe we can make it by tomorrow night!"

"Do you really think so? Then we can send Lyalus to your kingdom to get help! Your father can send his soldiers to save my family!" Porkita clapped her hands together in excitement.

"Let's try to go as far as we can today, so maybe we can be there by tomorrow, agreed?"

"Agreed!" answered Porkita.

They refilled their water bottles and set off along the river's edge, keeping constant watch for the arch made of trees. The afternoon passed and still they hadn't found it. Finally, through the shadows of dusk, they spied the arch. Grinning at each other, they clasped hands and raced the short distance to the arch, dancing beneath its spidery boughs.

When they stopped to catch their breath and eat a quick meal, Isabella asked, "Are you tired? Do you want to stop here for the night?"

"I am tired, but I think we should go further. Let's go until we can't take another step so we can reach the village of Teoli by tomorrow night," suggested Porkita.

Isabella agreed. The field they had to cross next was wide, but already lit by moonlight. High grass waved softly in the evening breeze. The girl's feet were heavy as they made their way to the center of the field. Suddenly, the hair on the back of Isabella's neck stood up and she froze.

"What's wrong, Isabella?" asked Porkita, alarmed.

"I don't know. I have this feeling someone's watching us. Let's hurry!"

Right then, rising up from the grass and charging at them from both sides were lines of the hideous soldiers. Isabella grabbed Porkita's hand and tried to run, but pointed spears immediately surrounded them. The girls shrank from the weapons and from the repulsive faces of the soldiers. Some of the soldiers looked like the one in the palace kitchen. But others had deep red skin and long narrow snouts or dark brown skin and hooded eyes. Everywhere Isabella looked, she saw a different kind of creature. The wall of warriors parted slightly and there before them, in his scarlet uniform, stood the one called Rankton.

"Princess Isabella," he roared, "how nice to meet you at last!" Rankton had a snout and a curly tail like the citizens of Sowden, but he was much larger, and his skin was mottled brown instead of pink. His eyes didn't have the warm shine Isabella always found in the eyes of the royal family, either. His were beady and hard. Coarse hair sprouted from his ears and cheeks.

A weary and frightened Isabella looked up at her massive enemy. "What do you want from us?"

"What do I want?" taunted Rankton. "Not much, Your Highness. Just the power to rule all that I see. I am going to be the master of all that roams the land and now that I have found you, you are going to help me." His snout quivered in excitement.

"Me? Why me? I don't even know you!"

"Ah, but I know you, Your Highness. I know all about you and have spent months planning for this meeting. But, first things first. Tie their hands behind their backs. We will leave this open area and find a secluded place to set up camp for the night before we have our little discussion," he ordered.

The soldiers did as he commanded and tied Isabella and Porkita's hands tightly behind their backs. They roughly pushed them into the wooded area by the river. There were tears streaming down Porkita's face. Isabella glanced back, heartbroken by how close they had come to reaching Teoli.

Rankton led the group to a grove sheltered by thick bushes and trees. Rankton bellowed orders until a fire was lit, food was prepared, and guards were posted around the edge of the campsite. Isabella and Porkita were told to sit on a log near the fire. Isabella dreaded the moment Rankton would finish giving orders and turn his attention back to her. Once everything was set up to his satisfaction, he sat down across from them and stared at Isabella, a nasty smirk on his face.

"Now, Your Highness, it's time to have a little talk. If you tell me what I want to know, you, your friend and your families will go free. If you refuse, you will be placing all of your lives in danger. Do you understand?"

"I understand what you are saying, but I don't understand what you want from me," insisted Isabella.

"All will become clear, Princess. Allow me to explain." Rankton settled back on the log and dug the heels of his great black boots into the dirt. His expression grew even harder as he spoke.

"My father was a great warrior. He was chief adviser to Hogden's father, who was an incompetent fool just like Hogden. My father knew the path to true leadership, only Hogden's father wouldn't listen. He was happy with the little world he ruled, as long as there was plenty of food on his plate. He couldn't see beyond his stomach! So my father passed the legend on to me. I tried to convince Hogden that he could command all creatures if he would only listen to me, but he, too, is only interested in stuffing food into himself. He actually told me that as long as the people of his kingdom were happy and well fed, he was satisfied! How could anyone be satisfied with that when he could be king of all the land? To have complete domination over every creature! Only an idiot would refuse an opportunity like that! And Hogden is an idiot."

Porkita's eyes lit up as she realized Hogitha's fiancé wasn't involved in Rankton's evil scheme.

Rankton continued, "So I took matters into my own hands. I began to form an army made up of all the outcasts from the Kingdom of Sowden. All the guards Hogden had kicked out because they didn't agree with his sissy ideas. 'Treat the subjects well and they will respect you,' he used to say. Subjects don't respect you because you treat them well; they respect you because they are afraid not to! My soldiers understand this as well as I do. And they wanted a leader who wasn't afraid to rule with an iron hoof! They know I'm that leader. Word spread and soon outcasts from villages and kingdoms all over the land were slinking into Sowden to join my army. They know that soon I will rule over everything, and they want to be by my side."

Isabella flinched from the madness glittering in Rankton's eyes.

"What does any of this have to do with me?" she asked again.

"I will be happy to explain, Princess. You see, the legend my father passed on to me was about a necklace, a gold necklace with a large star-shaped purple stone in the center. This necklace gives the one wearing it power over every other living creature. It vanished many years ago. It was rumored that it was taken by a tribe who chose to abandon all of us that live on the surface and make a new life for themselves under-ground. It hasn't been seen since. Until," his eyes burned even brighter as he leaned toward Isabella, "until you, Princess Isabella. One of my allies is close to your father. In fact, he is your father's chief medical adviser."

"Slyler?"

"That's right. He was growing weary of your father's way of ruling. Your father doesn't know the first thing about running a kingdom. Spending his days listening to all those subjects whine and complain about their petty problems! A true ruler shouldn't be bothered with the problems of the inhabitants of his kingdom! I ordered Slyler to stay close to your father and gather information that might be useful. Little did I know he would come across the most important, most precious piece of information possible."

Rankton leaned close to Isabella as though he was about to share a secret. A dark, dank odor surrounded Rankton, and Isabella was sure it was evil seeping through his very hide. "On the night you returned to the palace after your unfortunate kidnapping, you told your parents about your adventures. They in turn told Slyler and asked his advice. He advised them to have you keep silent, to tell no one what you had been through. At first, they took that advice. Slyler then came to me and described your travels. And that was when I knew you would lead me to the necklace."

Rankton rubbed his large hands together. "Unfortunately, your parents changed their feeble minds about letting you tell others what you had found, so we had to act quickly. When we learned you would be attending the wedding, Slyler put poison in your kingdom's water supply. Not enough to kill anyone, just enough to make them very ill. We sent messages to the other guests that the wedding was cancelled; then Slyler advised your parents to send you ahead alone so you wouldn't fall ill, too. That way I could grab you without your father's guards getting in the way. Your father trusts Slyler, fool that he is!"

"I don't know anything about any necklace. I never told anyone anything about a necklace," Isabella insisted.

"You still don't see it, do you? I thought you were smarter than that, Princess! You are going to take me to the underground village. You are going to lead me to the Garden of Robyia and help me take the necklace away from your friends, the Lanolions."

94

Chapter Seven

Let the Games Begin

Isabella gasped. "You think the Lanolions have this magic necklace? Why would you think that?"

"Didn't you tell your parents that you found a village inside of a mountain?"

"Yes, but that doesn't mean they are the ones who took the necklace! There could be other underground villages elsewhere. The Lanolions are gentle and peaceful. They wouldn't be interested in dominating other creatures."

"Maybe, maybe not. But this is the first underground village anyone has discovered, and I intend to find out if they have the necklace. Did you see anything while you were there that would make you think they have the necklace? Anything at all?"

Isabella thought back to her visit with the Lanolions. She remembered falling through the side of the mountain and landing inside a large hollowed-out dome. She recalled Inius's face when he burst through the bushes and saw her there. He was shocked to see a creature from the outside and was repulsed by her appearance. She was shocked by his green skin, odd-shaped body, and horns. He gave her a robe to cover her face and led her to the hut where Trofmin, the chief of the village, waited. Trofmin demanded to know who she was and what she wanted. He walked around her, touching her hair and staring at her face. Isabella closed her eyes and pictured the imposing chief in her mind; that's when she remembered the glittering purple necklace that hung around his neck. The memory of it shimmering in the firelight stood out in her mind.

"Well? Was there any sign of the necklace in the Lanolions' village?" demanded Rankton.

"I don't remember everything about my journey. A lot of the memories are spotty," Isabella told him.

Rankton kicked the dirt with the toe of his boot. "I had hoped you had seen the actual necklace, but it could still be there. Maybe they keep it hidden, or maybe you just didn't notice it. We will leave for the Garden of Robyia in the morning; then we shall see if the Lanolions have what I'm looking for."

"There's a problem with your plan," Isabella informed him.

"What problem?" roared Rankton.

"I have no idea where the Lanolions live. I was lost and wandering when I stumbled upon their home. I could never find my way back there again."

"Oh, I think you can. Especially since the lives of your family and friends depend on it," threatened Rankton. "Now we are all going to get a good night's sleep so we can head out early in the morning. The sooner we find the Lanolions and I relieve them of the necklace, the sooner my soldiers will set your families free." With one last malevolent glance at the two girls, he joined a group of soldiers. One of the soldiers came over to the girls and pulled them to their feet. He led them to two bedrolls on the ground and pushed them down.

"Isabella," whispered Porkita, "How are we supposed to sleep with our hands tied like this?"

"I don't know," Isabella whispered back. "I can't sleep anyway. All I can do is worry about how I'm supposed to lead him to a place I can't remember! If I don't, he'll hurt our families. And if I should happen to stumble upon the village of the Lanolions, what then? Will Rankton kill all the peaceful Lanolions just to get what he wants? And then will he truly have power over all the creatures in the land? I can't help him do that!"

The soldiers settled down for the night and soon snores echoed through the camp. Isabella could hear the soft snorts that Porkita made in her sleep. The only ones still awake were the guards stationed around the edge of the glen and Isabella.

She lay awake long into the night trying to find a solution, twisting and turning from the discomfort of the ropes and from the frustration of feeling helpless. A slight movement near her feet made her freeze. Isabella stared at the bushes nearest her. She was sure she had seen one of the bushes move slightly closer to her. Shaking her head to clear her vision, she stared again. Again the bush inched toward her.

Twisting her body so her feet were positioned to kick anything that should leap out at her, she waited. Muscles tensed and cramping, she stayed at the ready during the long moments it took for the bush to draw near. When it was finally close enough to reach with her outstretched legs, she drew them back tighter and aimed. Just as she would have lashed out, a voice whispered, "Isabella! It's Lyalus!"

"Lyalus!" she gasped. "What are you doing here?"

"Rescuing you, little one. I was hunting when I saw the soldiers gathering. I followed to see what they were up to. When I saw them capture you and your friend, I waited until I could sneak in here and get you out." Lyalus's low voice rumbled from the bush, but Isabella still could not see his face.

"Oh, Lyalus, I'm so glad you are here! I was so scared! How did you get past the guards?"

"Slowly, very slowly. Besides, these guards were not picked for their intelligence. They were too busy scratching and spitting to notice a moving bush. Plenty of time to talk later. We have to get you and your friend out of here right away. Can you wake her without her making any noise?"

Isabella turned to nudge Porkita, then stopped. She rolled back toward Lyalus and said, "I can't, Lyalus. I have to stay with Rankton."

Lyalus was silent for a moment. Then, "Isabella, what are you talking about? Who is Rankton?"

Isabella tried to explain. "Rankton is the big one in the scarlet uniform. He's the leader. Lyalus, if I leave with you, Rankton will kill Porkita's family before we can get help to them. If I stay, you'll have time to go to my kingdom, warn my father that his head medical adviser, Slyler, is putting poison in our water supply, and have my father lead his troops to Sowden to rescue Porkita's family. Rankton is holding her whole family captive until I show him where the Lanolions' village is. If I go with you, he might go straight there and kill them all."

"Slow down, Isabella. Someone is poisoning your water supply?" asked Lyalus. One of the soldiers stirred in his sleep, and they both stayed quiet until he settled down.

"Let me try to explain," whispered Isabella. "My parents and I were supposed to visit Porkita's home for her sister's wedding. The day before we were to leave, people in our kingdom became ill. No one could figure out why they were so sick. My parents sent me ahead to the Kingdom of Sowden so I wouldn't become sick, too. They stayed behind to help our people. While I was at Sowden, Rankton and his soldiers came and captured the whole royal family except Porkita and me. We managed to escape. We found Mystic tied up in a shed. She gave us a map and told us to come to you."

Isabella took a quick breath. "Rankton captured us today and told us that he's searching for something he wants, and he thinks the Lanolions have it. He thinks that I can lead him to them. He said that he had my father's chief medical adviser, Slyler, put poison in our kingdom's water supply so our subjects would become ill and I would be sent ahead. If I don't lead him to the Lanolions, he threatened to kill both our families. Now do you understand?"

"I think so. How is it going to help if you stay here? Are you going to lead him to the Lanolions?"

"Never! In the first place, I have no idea where their village is. In the second place, if I did find my way back, he would probably harm the Lanolions and if he finds what he wants, he will have power over all of us!" Isabella whispered angrily.

"Then what are you planning to do?"

"I am going to let him believe that I am leading him to them, but I will really be taking him on a wild goose chase! That will give you time to reach my father, tell him about Slyler and the poison, and send him to Sowden with his troops to free Porkita's family. Then he can send Mystic to find us and free us from Rankton. Will you do this for me, Lyalus?"

"I don't want to leave you here with these monsters. Isn't there any other way?" Lyalus pleaded.

"I can't think of one. Don't worry, Lyalus, we will be fine. I will be careful and as long as Rankton thinks I am leading him to the Lanolions, he won't harm us. You'd better leave now before someone catches you. Thank you for everything, Lyalus."

"Since I can't think of any other solution, I will follow your plan. I don't like it, but I don't see another choice. I will hurry, Isabella, and hopefully your father and I will be coming to rescue you very soon." Lyalus reached from the bushes and squeezed her foot.

Isabella watched as the bush holding Lyalus painstakingly inched away into the other bushes. Several times she had to bite down on her tongue to keep from calling to Lyalus to come back and take her and Porkita far away from these horrible soldiers. Finally, when she could no longer tell which bush held Lyalus in the darkness, she allowed her eyes to float closed in sleep.

The next morning, a huge guard shook them roughly to wake them. Rankton ordered several of his soldiers to pass out fruit and vegetables to everyone for breakfast. Their hands were untied so they could eat, but Isabella was sickened to find the green apple handed to her was full of small brown worms. She glanced at Porkita to see if she had better luck and saw Porkita popping the last bite of a pear into her mouth. Isabella discreetly dropped the wormy apple behind the log she sat on. She reached for the knapsack Grammy had given them, but it wasn't where she had left it. Glancing around the camp, she spotted two soldiers digging through her pack and examining the contents.

Rankton strode over to Isabella and towered above her. "Well, Princess, have you made up your mind? Are you ready to stop being stubborn and show me where the Lanolions live, or will your family have to suffer because of you?"

Isabella hesitated and then answered, "I have decided to show you where the Lanolions live in order to save my family and all the others. But . . ."

"But what, Princess?"

"I was thinking, instead of dragging us all that way with you, I could draw a map showing the exact directions to the Garden of Robyia. Then you could let us go and reach the Lanolions quicker."

Rankton almost smiled before replying, "I'm sure you would like that, Princess! But I think I'll keep you and your little friend with us until I have the necklace safe in my hands. As long as you behave, I will leave your hands untied. Now let's get moving! Which way, Princess?"

Isabella sighed and pointed up the river in the direction she and Porkita had traveled the day before. Rankton ordered his troops to move out, assigning two guards to walk in front of the girls and two guards to follow behind them. Isabella waited until the guards were a few feet away from them before whispering to Porkita.

"Porkita! Don't look at me, just listen."

"What is it, Isabella?" Porkita whispered back.

"Lyalus snuck into the camp last night to rescue us," Isabella confided.

Porkita stopped dead in her tracks and faced Isabella. "What? Then why are we still here?"

Isabella took her friend's arm and pulled her forward. "Don't stop! Keep walking. Pretend like nothing is wrong!"

"Isabella! Why didn't Lyalus rescue us?"

"Because if we had disappeared in the night, Rankton would have rushed straight back to your palace and killed your family before we could send help! We have to stall him long enough for Lyalus to reach my family, explain to my father about the poison in the water, and send help to your kingdom."

"Why can't your father just send his soldiers here to kill Rankton and his goons? Then we could go home to my kingdom."

"Because Rankton must have left soldiers at your palace to guard your family. If even one of these soldiers escapes my father's guards, they could ride straight to your kingdom and order your family and your subjects to be killed. We have to be sure your family is safe first. Maybe my father has enough guards to send some to your kingdom and some to help us at the same time. I'm not sure. In the meantime, Rankton must believe I am leading him to the Lanolions. I plan to make the journey very interesting for him."

Porkita asked, "What do you mean?" But just then a hideous soldier passed them and pushed Isabella a few steps in front of Porkita with an order to keep quiet.

When they had reached the point where the river straightened, Rankton stopped and asked Isabella, "Which way, Princess?" Isabella pointed through the trees toward the boulder field.

Isabella glanced back at Porkita and winked. Porkita raised her eyebrows in confusion but didn't speak. When they reached the boulder field, Rankton stopped once more.

"Now what?" he asked.

"Now we cross that field of rocks," Isabella answered.

Rankton stepped forward but stopped when Isabella spoke. "Don't tell him the secret, Porkita!"

Turning toward her, Rankton demanded, "What secret?"

Isabella acted flustered. "There is no secret! I didn't say anything about a secret!"

Rankton moved toward Porkita and raised his huge fist. "You'll tell me the secret or your friend will suffer!" he roared.

Porkita's eyes widened with fear, and Isabella rushed to stop him. "I'll tell you! Just don't hurt her!"

Smiling over his easy victory, Rankton gloated, "That's more like it! Now, what is this secret you are trying to keep from me?"

Isabella pretended to be reluctant to answer. "It's just that you don't have to walk all the way across that big field of rocks. The rocks will carry you the whole way if you want them to."

"What do you mean the rocks will carry us?"

"It's true. You can sit on the rocks, and they will give you a ride to the other side." Isabella hung her head. "I'm sorry, Porkita, I know I shouldn't have told him the secret, but he would have hurt you if I didn't tell him."

"That's right," Rankton agreed, "I would have. And I will hurt you if you ever try to keep a secret from me again. I am now your master. You are no longer princesses; you are my prisoners. Don't try to match your intelligence against mine! You will always lose!" With an arrogant toss of his head, he strode over to the closest rock and kicked it. Nothing happened.

"Try another one," Isabella told him.

Rankton moved to the next rock and kicked it as hard as he could. The rock instantly rose up and closed its stony teeth around the end of Rankton's boot. Rankton squealed in pain and pulled until the rock let go. He hopped around in a circle, bellowing and howling while his soldiers watched helplessly.

Rankton turned toward them in all his fury and shouted, "You will pay for this, Princesses! You will pay dearly for this!"

Chapter Eight

Bridges to Cross

Isabella stepped in front of Porkita as Rankton advanced on them, his face contorted with fury. She held up her hands to shield the two of them, then tried to quickly diffuse his anger.

"Master!" she pleaded, "Please! I didn't know that would happen! We crossed this boulder field several days ago and nothing bit our feet! Maybe you shouldn't have kicked it."

Slightly appeased by being called Master by this former princess, Rankton still did not believe in her innocence.

"I think you knew it would respond viciously!" he roared, still rubbing the injured foot with one hand.

"Master, why would I risk it when you have all the power? One word from you and these soldiers will dispose of Porkita and me. It would be a foolish move indeed to do anything to anger you." Isabella bowed her head in submission.

Rankton's ego was just large enough to believe her words. His chest puffed out as he replied, "You would be wise to remember that fact, Isabella. I don't keep people around who anger me. Just ask my soldiers what I do to those who fail me." Porkita and Isabella glanced at the soldiers, who were shifting their feet nervously and trying to avoid Rankton's gaze.

Isabella swallowed hard and said, "Master, if you would return my backpack to me, I have some herbs that I think will soothe the pain in your foot."

Rankton studied Isabella for a moment before nodding to one of the guards. Immediately, he carried her backpack forward and dropped it at her feet. She told Rankton to remove his boot, then rummaged through the pack until she found the leaves she sought. Breaking the leaf open, she squeezed the gel into Rankton's hand and instructed him to rub it on the wound. He did so and sighed with the relief it gave him. After a moment, he put his boot back on and stood.

"We are not crossing that rock field!" Rankton bellowed. "We will go around." He limped forward, followed by his soldiers and the girls.

"Isabella!" Porkita hissed. "It will take forever to walk around the rocks! You should have told him the right way to ride the rocks so we wouldn't have to walk so far!"

"No, Porkita," Isabella whispered back. "We want it to take a long time. Anything we can do to stall gives Lyalus more time to reach my father."

It was twilight before they finished circling the rock field. What had taken Isabella and Porkita about fifteen minutes to cross last time had taken Rankton and his men hours to go around.

Rankton ordered his men to set up camp for the night. After a meager meal of vegetables, Isabella and Porkita were ordered to go to bed.

"My men will be standing guard. Do not try to escape," threatened Rankton.

As Isabella and Porkita curled up on the hard ground, Porkita whispered, "What are we going to do next to slow them down, Isabella?"

Isabella yawned, her whole body aching with exhaustion. "Tomorrow we'll introduce them to the spitting frogs." Porkita shuddered before rolling over. Soon Isabella heard the snorts and grunts that meant Porkita had fallen asleep.

The group woke early and had a quick breakfast of fruit before they set out. It took most of the morning to reach the swamp. At the edge, Rankton ordered his men to stop.

"Which way now, Princess?" he asked.

"We have to go around this swampy area. It shouldn't take more than the rest of the afternoon," Isabella answered innocently.

"We're not going to waste time going around!" Rankton barked. "It will be much quicker to go through the center. Let's go!"

"Wait!" cried Isabella.

"What is it?" growled Rankton. "Why don't you want us to go straight through the swamp? Is it because there is some unpleasantness waiting around the edge that you hoped to lead us to? Sorry, Princess, not this time!"

"I can't be sure what awaits you in the swamp, Master. I only know that it is safe to go around the edge. I asked you to wait because I wanted to request the robes in my backpack so Porkita and I could shield our faces from the sun. It is burning our skin. Soon we may become delirious from the heat and forget how to reach the home of the Lanolions."

Rankton stared at her for a moment, then signaled to the soldier carrying Isabella's pack. He brought it forward, and Isabella retrieved the robes from it.

Handing Porkita a robe, she said, "Cover all your exposed skin,

Porkita. You don't want to get *burnt* again." Porkita nodded to show she understood.

Rankton strode into the swamp followed by everyone else. They had only gone a few feet when the first soldier was hit by the stinging green ooze. Soon the swamp was full of screaming, stumbling soldiers. Some were crawling, their hands covering their faces. Others were running as fast as they could, only to be slowed by another burning, green missile. Rankton was desperately trying to restore order and dodge the ooze at the same time. Isabella and Porkita had linked arms under the robes and were steadily making their way across the swamp, protected from the burning spit. Isabella peeked out once to see Rankton darting left and right, stomping on bullfrogs with his heavy boots. Isabella saw one explode as he crushed it. She shuddered and let the robe drop closed again.

The princesses reached the other side of the swamp first and removed the robes, careful not to touch any of the slime coating the outside. As they waited, soldiers came bursting out through the reeds, frog spit dripping from them. Rankton was one of the last to exit, and the murderous look on his face was worse than the one when the rock bit him.

He stormed up to Isabella, wiping slime off his face with the back of his enormous hand. When his face was mere inches from hers, he stopped.

"Do you think this is some kind of game, Princess?" he asked, his voice filled with rage. Isabella could see the clusters of tiny blisters forming on his face where the venom had hit him and she remembered how strongly it burned.

"No, Master!" she quickly assured him. "I think what happened to you and your soldiers is horrible! Porkita and I were just fortunate to be protected by our robes, or we would be slimy like you! What were those awful things?"

Rankton stared hard into her eyes as he answered, "I think you know very well what those things were and just what they would do. Isn't it convenient that you requested your robes right before we entered the swamp?"

Isabella defended herself. "Yes, but I did tell you to go around the swamp since I knew that way was safe. I told you I wasn't sure if going straight through the swamp would be safe, didn't I, Master?"

Rankton grabbed Porkita roughly by the arm and dragged her to the edge of the swamp. Porkita squealed in fear.

"Perhaps you would change your attitude if I took your little friend for a nice walk through the swamp? Shall I? No?" He dropped Porkita's arm. "No more games, Isabella. You will take me to the land of the Lanolions, and there will be no more stalling and no more unpleasantness. Now fetch some of that medicine you put on my foot so my soldiers and I can have some relief!"

Isabella divided the medicine among the soldiers. There was some pushing and shoving, some arguing about who should be first to receive treatment, but once they all had ointment on their burns, the group gathered their possessions and moved on. They only traveled a short distance before Rankton told them to set up camp for the night. Isabella had noticed him limping and decided the injury to his foot must be bothering him.

A soldier threw some old fruit on the ground in front of the princesses and they ate it rapidly. Isabella watched as Rankton devoured a whole pot of what smelled like hot stew, then topped it off with three of Grammy's homemade muffins. The soldiers all were eating hot food, too, while Isabella and Porkita were half-starving on the little bit of overripe fruit and dirty vegetables they were given. It was especially hard on Porkita, who was used to eating almost constantly. Isabella watched Porkita eat her apple, core and all, and knew she was dreaming about the fine corn dishes she was used to enjoying.

When they could hear the soldiers' snores all around them, Porkita whispered, "What is the plan for tomorrow?"

Isabella replied, "I have no idea. If we keep retracing the same route, we will lead them right to Grammy's cabin. I can't do that. So I am going to have to take them into unknown territory. And if we run into any trouble, Rankton will think I planned it that way and will take it out on us."

"What if we go a different way and we accidentally lead them to the Lanolions?"

"That can't happen," Isabella assured her. "I have no idea where the Lanolions' home is and even if I stumbled upon it, it is hidden underground. I wouldn't even know I was on the mountain that hid the Garden of Robyia. And neither would Rankton." Isabella yawned and stretched. "We'd better get some sleep. Tomorrow will be another long day."

Isabella was awakened by a soldier's boot digging in her back. She turned and gently shook Porkita so she wouldn't suffer a similar fate. Porkita sat up, stretched, and then eagerly grabbed the fruit tossed on the ground in front of her. As she ate, Isabella watched Rankton storming around the camp, bellowing orders at his men. His mood seemed to be growing fouler every day.

"I told you I wanted it hot! Not warm, hot!" Rankton screamed at a soldier who was trailing after him, holding a wooden cup in his hands. Rankton turned and backhanded the soldier, knocking him and the cup to the ground. He gave the soldier a hard kick before striding away.

"Oh, Isabella," whispered Porkita, her breakfast forgotten for the moment, "don't do anything to make him angry today, okay?"

Isabella saw the small wooded area to her left and knew that it led first to a large open field and then straight to Grammy's cabin. To the right was unfamiliar territory.

"Which way, Princess?" asked Rankton.

"This way," she answered, pointing to the right. She swallowed hard, hoping she had made the right choice.

Isabella and Porkita struggled to keep up with Rankton and his soldiers. Stumbling over tree roots and vines, Porkita whispered, "I don't know how much longer I can go on, Isabella! I'm hot and exhausted. My feet hurt from walking, my back hurts from sleeping on the hard ground, and I'm starving! I have never been this hungry in my whole life! I can't take much more!"

Isabella looked over at her friend, normally so perfectly groomed and dressed. Porkita had dirt smeared on her face and twigs and leaves tangled in her hair. Her dress was not only torn and stained, but also hung a little loosely on her thinning body. Porkita looked as tired and as miserable as a creature can get, and Isabella knew she looked the same.

"I know, Porkita," answered Isabella in a low voice. "I feel the same way. I can't stop worrying about our families, and I have no idea what we are going to face in the next few days. I wish my father would hurry up and rescue us! I wonder if Lyalus reached my kingdom? Maybe they have already saved your family and are on their way to help us!"

"I hope they hurry!" mumbled Porkita. "I hope they find us before it is too late."

Isabella wanted to tell her everything would be okay, that they just had to be strong and hold on a little longer. But she was having trouble believing it herself. More than ever, Isabella wished she had run away with Lyalus that first night.

The group trudged on. Isabella's head drooped and her feet dragged across the ground. Each step became a challenge. With the sun baking her body, she lost track of time and direction. She no longer cared where they were going or why. Her mind skittered dangerously in all directions, visions of her childhood flooding it one moment, terrifying images of dark, hideous creatures crowding it in the next. And still they continued.

Isabella was brought back to reality when her head slammed into the soldier in front of her as he came to an abrupt stop. She glanced at Porkita and was alarmed to see a glazed, unfocused look in her eyes.

"Porkita!" she cried, shaking her friend's arm, but Porkita didn't respond.

The soldiers were drinking water from jugs, and Isabella grabbed one. She held the jug over Porkita's head and let the water pour down her friend's face. Then she held it to Porkita's lips and forced her to drink. At first, Porkita just let the water trickle out the sides of her mouth, but soon she was eagerly slurping it. When her thirst was quenched, she handed the jug back to Isabella, and Isabella drank her fill. Isabella also splashed some on her own face, which helped to clear her mind a bit.

A soldier from the front of the line pushed his way through the group until he reached the girls. He grabbed them by their arms and pulled them back through the crowd. As they broke through the cluster of soldiers, Isabella saw that they were standing on the edge of a large canyon. The canyon was deep and the rock walls were too steep to climb down easily.

"Well, Isabella," Rankton asked, "how did you cross this on your journey?"

Isabella scrambled to find an answer, desperately trying not to reveal that she had never even seen this place before, much less crossed it. As she searched for a solution, her eyes scanned the canyon walls looking for anything that might help.

"Well, Isabella, I'm waiting for an answer."

"I-I-I didn't cross here. I mean, I crossed farther down. We need to walk along the edge of the canyon until we reach the spot where I crossed. But could we please have something to eat first? Porkita and I won't be able to continue unless we have some nourishment. We're too weak."

"Fine. Give Isabella two pieces of fruit and some dried meat. I'll never find the necklace if she starves to death! But nothing for the other one. She is no use to me and I won't waste our supplies on her!"

Isabella stood tall and stuck out her quivering chin. "If you don't give Porkita the same amount as you give me, I'll give her my food. Then I'll starve to death anyway, and you'll never find your necklace!"

"You dare threaten me!" roared Rankton, and the soldiers drew back in fear.

"I'm not threatening you. I'm telling you that I won't eat and watch my best friend starve! So if you want me to help you, you have to take care of Porkita, too."

Rankton glared for another moment before stiffly saying, "Fine. Give the other one the same. We will all stop here for a bit and have a meal. Break out the supplies! Wormer! Fix me something to eat! And make it quick!" The soldier called Wormer scurried to obey as Rankton stomped away.

Porkita and Isabella sank to the ground, relieved to rest their tired bodies. Porkita peeled off her fancy slippers and rubbed her blistered feet, while Isabella fanned herself with her skirt. A soldier came with their food; for the first time, it was handed to them instead of thrown at their feet. Isabella traded her fruit for Porkita's meat, since Porkita was a vegetarian. The girls eagerly ate everything. It was more than they had eaten in a long while, but they were both still famished. Isabella asked for a jug of water and received it. After another long drink, while they still didn't feel well, they felt better than they had all day.

"Where are you leading them now?" Porkita asked, as she checked the nearby bushes for any edible berries.

"I have no idea. I've never been here before," Isabella whispered. "I hope we find somewhere safe to cross soon, or Rankton will figure out that I'm leading him on a wild goose chase."

"If he figures that out, we're in big trouble. Are these leaves safe to eat?"

"No, they're not," answered Isabella, watching the soldiers stuff themselves with food. "Try to think of the wonderful feast we will have when we are all safe at the palace! Your family and my family sitting down together to celebrate our triumph over Rankton! Won't that be a joyous occasion?"

Porkita's eyes grew as large as plates. "Will there be corn fritters? And corn pancakes? And lots of steaming hot corn soup?"

Isabella laughed. "All that you can eat before you burst! And once we are home, I promise, you will never be without food again!"

Porkita laughed, too, and then leaned over to hug her good friend.

At Rankton's order, the soldiers gathered up their things and the girls got to their feet. The group headed along the edge of the canyon, each passing moment increasing Isabella's anxiety. As the sun began to sink in the sky, she heard a loud shout and was sure Rankton had caught on to her lies, especially when she and Porkita were passed to the front of the line again.

But Rankton didn't look murderous when she reached his side. He looked almost pleased.

"How right you were, Isabella!" he crowed. "This will make our crossing much easier!"

Isabella looked toward the canyon and had to fight to keep her mouth from dropping open. There before her was a bridge constructed of rope and wooden planks extending clear to the opposite side. She made sure her face was devoid of all expression.

"I'm glad you are pleased, Master," she answered, hating the bitter taste that filled her mouth every time she called him by that title.

"I am very pleased, Isabella, that you are finally finished playing games and that you have realized that I *am* your master. And with your help, soon I will be master of all that lives! But just to be on the safe side . . ."

He grabbed Porkita roughly by the arm. "I think your fat friend here will cross first. To prove this isn't another one of your tricks. If she makes it across safely, the rest of us will follow."

Amid Isabella's protests and Porkita's frightened squeals, he grabbed a spear from one of his men and prodded Porkita in the back with it. Keeping up the pressure, he forced her onto the rickety bridge.

Porkita's first step caused the bridge to swing and sway, and she screeched loudly.

"Calm down, Porkita!" Isabella yelled. "Just go slowly and hold on the sides! You'll be fine, I promise!" Even as she tried to convince Porkita, Isabella felt her heart pound with fear. Over Porkita's squeals came the sound of the bridge creaking as it swayed high above the canyon floor. A chunk of something broke free from the bridge and spun wildly through the air before splintering into pieces as it hit the ground.

Isabella thought her heart would stop. "Porkita!" she screamed. "Hold on tight! Don't let go!"

Rankton gave the spear another jab, forcing Porkita forward another step. She screamed and gripped the rope sides.

"Go ahead, Porkita! It's better if you go on your own instead of being pushed!"

Porkita took a tentative step forward. The bridge creaked but held. Another small step. Two more. Then a little more confidently, Porkita moved slowly forward until she was halfway across.

She turned to call, "I'm okay, Isabella," and the wood beneath her left foot gave way, sending her left leg plunging through the ropes.

Isabella screamed as Porkita struggled to pull herself back up. Then

Isabella darted past Rankton and onto the swaying bridge.

"Get her," Rankton bellowed as Isabella quickly made her way to her friend. She helped Porkita pull her leg out of the hole and the two friends embraced. The bridge bounced dangerously as some of Rankton's soldiers started across.

"Follow me," Isabella told Porkita. She turned and continued toward the opposite wall. "I'm not sure this bridge can hold our weight and theirs. We should hurry."

The soldiers were cautious in their pursuit, despite Rankton's orders to move faster. The girls were almost to the other side, and the soldiers had only reached the center.

There was a loud groaning as the bridge tore in half. Isabella and Porkita were left hanging from the frayed ropes several feet from the edge of the cliff. They watched as a half dozen soldiers fell to the canyon floor. Hauling herself up hand-over-hand, Isabella managed to reach solid ground. She quickly turned and helped Porkita. Once on their feet, they looked across the wide canyon to see Rankton bellowing and shaking his fist in the air.

Chapter Nine

Princesses Don't Spit

"What are we going to do now?" Porkita cried.

"Run!" yelled Isabella, as she grabbed her friend's hand and tugged.

The two girls ran breathlessly through the brush, putting as much distance between them and Rankton as possible. When they could run no further, they collapsed on the ground, holding their sides as they gasped for air.

"I-uh-I-uh-I don't understand!" Porkita panted. "I thought we had to stay with Rankton to protect our families. Otherwise, we could have escaped with Lyalus days ago!"

"I know, but Rankton will know something's not right if we don't try to escape. And maybe we gave Lyalus enough time to reach my father and send troops."

"But what if we didn't?" whined Porkita.

"I don't know, Porkita!" Isabella snapped. "I don't have all the answers. I just know that I'm tired, I want a bath, and I want something to eat!"

Porkita had never heard Isabella talk like this before. "I'm sorry, Isabella. It's okay. Your father's troops are probably looking for us right now. Let's find food and a place to bathe. Then we'll be able to think clearer."

"I'm sorry, too, Porkita. I didn't mean to yell at you. I'm just so tired, and I don't know what the right thing to do is anymore. I want my mother and father." Isabella's shoulders drooped and Porkita put her arm around her friend.

The two girls walked through the brush looking for any sign of food or water. The sun set, but the moon was bright, so they were able to find several berry bushes and five pears within their reach. They stuffed the food in their mouths as they continued to look for water. They finally found a small creek and collapsed beside it, drinking deeply and splashing water on their faces and arms.

Isabella sat back and wiped her mouth. "I think we should sleep here tonight. I don't think I can take another step. In the morning, we can figure out what we should do next. Is that all right with you?" At Porkita's nod, Isabella glanced around at their surroundings. "Let's pull some of these branches into a pile and make a bed. I can't take another night of sleeping on the bare ground! I would give anything to have Grammy's pack right now. I miss those big fluffy quilts."

The girls wearily broke off some of the softer branches and dragged them into a sheltered spot within the brush. They dropped onto the pile and were swiftly asleep.

Awakened by the sound of birds chattering, Isabella was surprised to see how high the sun was. She stretched and sat up, feeling more rested than she had in days. Looking at Porkita's peaceful face and hearing her gentle snores, Isabella decided not to wake her until she could find something for their breakfast.

Pushing her way through the brush, Isabella found a bush loaded with berries and a tree with some small apples. She filled her skirt with them, then returned to where Porkita slept. She built a small fire around a stone with an indentation in the top. She mashed the fruit and put it into the indentation, added a little water from the creek, and as the stone heated up, so did the fruit.

Isabella was just about to wake Porkita when she sat up and asked,

"Do I smell something cooking or am I still dreaming?"

Isabella grabbed two thick leaves, handed one to Porkita, and using them as spoons, the girls dug into the stewed fruit. There was plenty, and the first warm meal they had eaten in days filled their stomachs and revived them.

"So (lick) what do you (lick) want to (slurp) do now?" asked Porkita, thoroughly enjoying the last drops of fruit.

"I thought about it while I was gathering fruit this morning. I told Lyalus we should stay with Rankton because he would have no reason to harm our families as long as he had me. After all, the only thing he was interested in was what I knew about the Lanolions. And I believed Rankton wouldn't harm us as long as we cooperated. I didn't plan to escape, it just happened."

Isabella paused. She didn't want to frighten her friend. "But I no longer believe Rankton won't harm us. If we let Rankton recapture us, he might end up killing you. He risked your life on the bridge and he didn't even care. He was also ready to starve you to death. And when he figures out that I'm not leading him to the Lanolions, he will probably kill me, too. We can't count on my father finding us before that happens."

Porkita agreed. "I don't want to let Rankton find us, either. I think we gave Lyalus a good head start, and if your father and his troops aren't already at my kingdom, they soon will be. I think we should avoid Rankton. Maybe he'll be too busy looking for us to go to our kingdoms and harm our families."

"I don't think so. I think he will immediately send troops to both our kingdoms to wait in case we make our way there. Hopefully, my father will have soldiers stationed to protect our people. But we can't go back to our kingdoms, just in case," reasoned Isabella. "I also think Rankton and some of his men will be hunting for us."

"So what do you think we should do?"

Isabella looked her straight in the eye. "I think we should avoid being found by Rankton. Meanwhile, we should try to find the home of the Lanolions and warn them about him."

"How are we going to do that?" asked Porkita, wide-eyed.

"We'll have to be very careful. We can't leave a trail for him to follow. It will take him awhile to find a new way across the canyon, so we can get ahead of him. And then we just have to stay way ahead of him," explained Isabella.

"But you said you have no idea where the Lanolions live! So how can we find them?"

"We'll have to retrace the route I took on my first journey and just hope we are very lucky."

"Where do we start?" asked Porkita.

"Grammy's cabin," Isabella replied. "It's a good place to start, and Grammy can help us replace the supplies Rankton took from us."

"What if Rankton has sent men there again?"

"We'll sneak in at night. We'll disguise ourselves. I don't know what we'll do, but somehow we'll find a way. Are you ready?"

"Do you know how to get to Grammy's house from here?" asked Porkita.

"No. But I know how to get there if we can get back across this canyon. I'm sure Rankton is hurrying around the edge of the canyon to get to this side to catch us, so if we can find a way to get back to that side, not only will we be on the right path to Grammy's house, but we will also be escaping Rankton."

"Can we get across without the bridge? It looked pretty steep!" observed Porkita.

"Let's go take a look. But we have to be careful in case Rankton found a way across and is already on this side."

They quietly and carefully made their way back through the brush until they reached the edge of the canyon. The brush was so thick that they didn't realize they were at the canyon's edge until they almost fell into it. Luckily, they didn't end up at the exact same spot as the day before, so they didn't see the broken bridge or the soldiers' bodies.

"Can we climb down here?" asked Porkita.

"I don't think so. Even if we could get down, we could never get up that other side, and I don't want to be trapped in the canyon if Rankton comes along. We'll have to follow the edge until we find a spot where we can get in and back out again."

"Which way?"

Isabella thought for a moment. "Well, to the right will take us closer to Grammy's, but that's probably the way Rankton and his men went. So, I think we should go to the left. What do you think?"

"I think anything that takes us farther away from Rankton and his goons is the right way to go!"

It was well into the afternoon before Isabella found the spot she was looking for. She paced back and forth staring at the rock walls while Porkita rested on the ground.

"I think this will work," announced Isabella.

"How?"

"We'll need a couple of long vines. And it won't be easy. But I think we can do it." She strode off into the trees, returning shortly dragging the vines.

"This is going to be complicated, Porkita. We'll have to lower ourselves down these vines. It will be a little dangerous, and you'll have to be steady on your feet. Do you think you can do it?"

"If I could cross that horrible bridge, I can do anything. Let's go!"

Porkita answered with more conviction than she felt.

Isabella secured Porkita's vine to a tree and then threw it over the cliff. She did the same with her own vine.

"Now Porkita, just slowly lower yourself down the wall. You can use your feet to steady yourself against the wall. Okay?"

Porkita nodded and then watched as Isabella lowered herself over the edge.

"See, Porkita! It's easy!" she called. "Just take it nice and slow."

"Whee-e-e-e!" Porkita flew past Isabella, sliding rapidly down her vine. Isabella looked down to see Porkita land with a crash on the floor of the canyon. She stood up and brushed off her skirt before yelling, "Come on, Isabella! Why are you taking so long?"

Isabella speeded up her descent a little, but did not fly down the way Porkita did. When she reached the bottom, Isabella landed smoothly on her feet.

"Porkita! Are you all right? You were supposed to come down slowly," exclaimed Isabella.

"Why? I'll bet my way was more fun!" Isabella just shook her head as they headed across the floor of the canyon.

Once they reached the other side, Isabella attempted to explain to Porkita how they were going to climb out. "I'll get down on my hands and knees and you step on my back and climb onto the boulder, then reach down and pull me up."

So Isabella knelt down and Porkita stepped onto her back. Then Porkita pulled herself up onto the first boulder. Once there, she was able to lay down on the edge and reach Isabella's hand to hoist her up. They continued this way, boulder after boulder until they reached the top. Both girls flopped on the ground, sweaty, dirty, and exhausted, with every muscle aching from the effort.

"We made it," said Isabella, between gulps of air.

"Yes," agreed Porkita, "but let's not do that again, all right?"

"Definitely not."

After they had rested briefly they made their way back through the thick underbrush that they had come through with Rankton and his men the day before. The going was slow because of the dense tangle of bushes and because they tried to move quietly. It took them until sunset to pass through the brush and reach the edge of the swamp.

"We are going to stop for the night now, aren't we?" Porkita practically begged.

Isabella looked at her bedraggled friend and sighed. "I think we should keep going if we can. I know you're tired. I am, too, but Grammy's house isn't far, and we should arrive in the middle of the night so there is less of a chance of leading Rankton there. Besides, you don't want to camp this close to the spitting frogs, do you?" At

Porkita's disgruntled look, Isabella added, "Grammy has soft beds and the most delicious food . . ."

Porkita visibly perked up. "What are we standing here for? Let's get moving!" And she marched off.

Isabella smiled before calling, "It's this way, Porkita!"

As tired as they were, at least it was easier traveling in the cool of the evening. Knowing that they were going to be at Grammy's cabin also gave them a bit of energy. Still, it took several hours and the moon was high in the sky by the time Isabella spotted the cabin in the distance. They moved through the fruit trees until they were close enough to see the doorway.

"We can't just walk up to the cabin," said Isabella. "What if Rankton has men waiting to see if we show up here?"

"We could crawl up without being seen," suggested Porkita.

"I think they would see us. If there were bushes near the house, then maybe, but there is too much wide open space."

"But we have to do something soon! I'm hungry and exhausted, my feet hurt and I'm hungry." Porkita was getting a whiney note in her voice again.

Isabella was too tired to come up with a plan. She was staring at the cabin, thinking, when she saw a movement through the curtains. There it was again! Suddenly a great, majestic bird flew out the open window and soared over their heads.

"Orion! Orion!" Isabella hissed, trying to draw his attention without attracting anyone else's.

The bird made two large sweeps of Grammy's property before gliding into land gently on Isabella's outstretched arm.

"Hello, pretty Orion," Isabella cooed, softly stroking his feathers. "Porkita, can you tear off a small piece of my slip? I want to write Grammy a note."

"We can use a piece of mine this time," she answered, ripping a small strip from it.

"Can you write and ask Grammy if it's safe to come in?"

"I'll try," answered Porkita. "What should I use to write with?"

"Well, I'm guessing your candy stick is all gone?"

Porkita nodded sheepishly.

"Then spit in the dirt to make a little mud and use that."

Porkita's face was a picture of horror. "Spit! You want me to spit? I've never spit in my life! Princesses don't spit!"

"Do you want to get inside to Grammy's cooking and nice soft beds or not?"

Porkita thought hard for a moment, then said, "Well, at least look the other way. I don't want you to see me do it." Isabella smiled and turned away.

A few moments later, Porkita asked, "How is this?" Isabella looked at the strip of cloth and saw that Porkita had written, "Iz it saf? Izzabela."

"I'm sure Grammy will know what we mean," Isabella reassured her. "Orion, take this to Grammy! Take it to Grammy!" The large bird took the scrap in his mouth and flew toward the cabin. The girls waited restlessly, until finally they saw the front door open and the little old lady wave at them to come forward.

"Let's go quickly, just in case anyone is watching," Isabella suggested.

"The quicker, the better, as far as I'm concerned," agreed Porkita before sprinting across the open yard followed closely by Isabella.

"Come in! Come in, children!" called Grammy from the doorway. She waited until they were safely inside, then closed and latched the door.

Grammy turned and took Isabella in her arms for a long hug. "Oh, it's good to see you, child! I've bin so worried about you two." She let go of Isabella only to sweep Porkita into her arms. Porkita's eyes watered at the kindness from the old lady, and her mouth watered at the delicious food smells wafting through the cabin.

Grammy wiped her eyes with the corner of her apron, gave Isabella another quick squeeze, and then said, "Come sit a spell, and we'll gnaw back while you tell me what you've bin up to. The two of you look half-starved and as puny as a long-tailed swamp rat!"

Porkita's eyes lit up as Isabella responded, "We are really hungry, Grammy, and would appreciate something to gnaw. But first, we need to know if you have seen any more of those soldiers who were looking for us?"

"Naw! Those varmints haven't bin back since you was here before. They probably knowed Orion and I would take the skin right off 'em if they showed their ugly pusses round here agin!" Grammy got so excited she slammed the butter dish onto the table. "Are they still chasin' you girls?" She sliced thick pieces of bread from a loaf.

"Actually, they caught us," Isabella informed her. "Soon after we left here last time. We were their prisoners until we escaped yesterday."

"Oh, you poor, poor children! Did ya ever find out what they wanted from ya?"

"They want me to lead them to the Lanolions. Do you remember me telling you about Inius and the Lanolions when I came here the first time?"

"Sakes, yes! Weren't they the earth dwellers? The ones who lived inside the mountain?"

"That's them," Isabella told her. "Rankton thinks they have something that will give him power over all living creatures, so naturally he wants it. He wants me to lead him to it."

"A rotter like that with power over everyone? That would be the end of decent folk fer sure! Thank the stars you got away from him! Are ya headed fer home now?"

"No, Grammy. We are trying to retrace the path I took when I escaped from Malachi and see if we can find the Lanolions to warn them."

"Ya cain't do that, Isabella! It's too dangerous! Ya have to git home to your folks where ya'll be safe!"

"But Grammy, if Rankton finds the Lanolions on his own, no one will be safe! I have to warn them!"

Isabella heard a gulp behind her and turned to see Porkita staring wild-eyed at the table which was now laden with Grammy's food.

Hungry herself, Isabella asked, "Do you think we could eat while we talk, Grammy?"

"Sakes, yes! I'm sorry, girls. I weren't thinking. Sit and gnaw back all ya want! Help yerself!"

Porkita nearly tripped in her hurry to reach the table. She grabbed a thick slice of bread, smeared a heavy layer of jam on it and crammed it into her mouth. She sighed contentedly before reaching for a second slice, globs of jam dotting her face.

Isabella also took a slice of bread and added jam. She ate it slower than Porkita, but not by much. Grammy had also set out tall glasses of fruit juice, some dried meat, and stewed apples.

Porkita's mouth was full as she asked, "Grammy, this is all (slurp) wonderful (swallow), but would you happen to have any corn?"

"Corn? Ya want corn? Nobody in these here parts grows corn like Grammy does!" She opened a large cupboard and thick, ripe ears of corn came tumbling out.

Porkita's eyes lit up and she flew to the cupboard to help herself to several ears. With Porkita happily munching her corn, Isabella was able to continue her conversation with Grammy.

"Do you think it would be all right if we stayed here for the night, Grammy?" asked Isabella.

"'Course it would! You girls need yer rest and ya'll think better in the lighttime. Orion will keep an eyeball on things and let us know if'n there is trouble comin'. Meantimes, ya better gnaw a little more and put some paddin' on yer racks afore you blow clean away!"

Porkita stopped eating for a moment and wrinkled her forehead in confusion, then shrugged and went back to eating her corn. Isabella just smiled as she stood up and gave Grammy a hug.

"You are the best, Grammy! Thank you so much for everything. I really wish my parents could meet you! Once we are safely home, do you think you could come visit us? I'm sure my father would send his carriage and a squad of soldiers to escort you comfortably to our kingdom."

"Me in a royal carriage? Visiting a king and queen? Did ya ever hear of such a thing? I would be as proud as a wofty sittin' on a nestful of eggs!"

Grammy gave Isabella another squeeze, then said, "If'n ya are done gnawin', I'll fix yer bunks so's ya kin git some sleep." Porkita reluctantly put down her fifth ear of corn, yawned, and followed Grammy.

Grammy turned down the thick comforters on the two single beds and the girls eagerly crawled in.

"But, Grammy," Isabella asked, struggling to keep her eyes open, "where will you sleep?"

"Hush, child! Don't worry about Grammy. I'll sleep in my rocker like I do lots of darktimes. I'll be right comfortable. Close them eyes and rest."

Isabella heard the rustle of Orion's wings as he flew out the window to stand guard. She gave into her exhaustion and slept deeply, waking only once when she heard loud crunching noises. She tensed, expecting to find Rankton standing over her, but was relieved to find it was only Porkita enjoying a middle-of-the-night snack. Isabella reassured herself that Grammy was dozing peacefully in her rocker, then curled under the comforter for a few more hours of sleep.

Chapter Ten

Unseen Danger

The delicious aroma of Grammy's cooking woke Isabella. She saw Grammy bent over the fireplace, stirring a pot of something and Porkita sitting at the table, waiting impatiently.

"Good morning!" Isabella called as she threw off the comforter and joined them in the kitchen area.

"Good lighttime, child! Did ya sleep well?" Grammy asked.

"Best sleep I've had in a very long time, thank you. I feel bad about taking your bed, though. Did you get any sleep at all?"

"Don't bother about Grammy; my old bones sleep better sittin' up anyhow. I've got fresh-made muffins, bread, and stewed fruit. Are ya ready to gnaw back?"

"I am," replied Porkita, reaching for a corn muffin.

"Me, too," agreed Isabella.

As the girls dug into the delicious breakfast, talk turned to their plan. "Are ya sure ya should go looking for these earth dwellers? That Rankton might be on ya quicker than ants on an ogler! Shouldn't ya jus' go home?"

"We have to give Lyalus time to reach my kingdom and alert my father to the danger. Then my father's troops can capture Rankton's men and save Porkita's family. If we go home now, Rankton's men will be waiting for us, and we'll all be trapped. Once Lyalus and my father have defeated the enemy, they will come and find us and bring us safely home," explained Isabella.

"You could be awandering for many lighttimes and not find those lion things! How bout ifn ya stay here and wait fer yer father and Lyalus?" offered Grammy.

"Rankton will look for us here, and I won't put you and Orion in any more danger! As much as I would love to spend time with you, Grammy, I think we should leave this morning in case Rankton is in the area."

"But, Isabella," Porkita protested through a mouthful of muffin, "can't we stay here just for a little while? Maybe just until tomorrow? Just until we are rested and full?"

"I'd love to stay, Porkita. I'm tired of walking, and I'm tired of being hungry, too. But we have to stay ahead of Rankton, and we can't put Grammy in danger. I think we should leave as soon as we finish eating. Is that all right with you?" asked Isabella.

Porkita looked at all the delicious food on the table in front of her, then reluctantly nodded her agreement.

"Don't you worry none, Porkita. I'll fix ya a big sack of my cookin' to take with ya," Grammy promised. Porkita cheered up immediately. Grammy asked, "Do ya wanna have a quick wash-down fore ya go? I can heat some water fer ya."

Porkita looked at Isabella longingly. Isabella couldn't deny that she wanted a bath as much as Porkita did.

"That would be wonderful, Grammy. We had better be quick, though."

While the water heated over the fire, Grammy dug through her trunks once again and found two plain dresses for the girls to put on once they had bathed. She also found two more quilts and some basic supplies, tying them into a bundle for the girls to take with them. Once the water boiled, she poured it into a large metal tub that stood in the corner of the sleep area, then added some cold water and flower blossoms.

"My manmate, Thomas, brought this back fer me. He was always bringing me doodads that he traded fer on his travels. But when he brought this back, I thought he'd near lost his mind! 'What am I supposed to cook in that pot?' I asked him. He says, 'It's not fer cooking, it's fer washing yerself. You fill it with water and git in it.' I thought he were crazy! I jest let it sit there a couple of lighttimes, and wouldn't try it no matter how he tried to sweet-talk me into it."

Grammy blushed. "Then he left on another trip and my curiosity got me. I dragged it out and filled it with nice, warm water. I taked off my robe, and, feelin' like a dang fool, I climbed in. Well, if'n it weren't nicer than a walk in the moon-glow, I don't know what! After that, you couldn't hardly git me outta that dang thing! I used it all the time! It were a lot nicer than splashing in that cold creek to git clean, that's fer sure."

Grammy filled the tub halfway and then said, "Porkita-child, I'm a gonna pull this curtain over and you hop on into that tub! I laid a cloth fer washing and a bigger cloth fer drying on the chair there and there is some sweet soap there fer scrubbing. Made it myself with flowers from my garden. I put some extree in your pack so's you can use it when you are in them cold rivers. You take yer time and have a nice wash-down, ya hear?"

Porkita nodded, and then gave Grammy an impulsive hug before slipping behind the curtain.

"I hope it were okay fer me to let her go first, Isabella. It seemed like it meant more to her. 'Sides I think this adventure has bin tougher on her than you. You bin through this here kinda thing before and came out stronger than the stink on a skunk."

Isabella smiled. "It's fine, Grammy. You are right, this has been very hard on Porkita. Besides, this way I can have time to chat with you while Porkita bathes-er-has a wash down."

Grammy and Isabella had a cup of tea and talked about Isabella's life since her return to the palace. Grammy filled Isabella in on what she and Orion had been up to since Isabella's first visit. Occasionally, they would hear splashes and sighs of contentment from behind the curtain and they both would smile.

Finally, when Isabella could put it off no longer, she called, "Porkita? Are you almost ready to get out?"

"No."

"You aren't finished washing yet?"

"No."

"Isn't the water getting cold?"

"No."

"When do you think you'll be finished?"

There was a little pause, and then, "I'm not coming out."

"I know you are enjoying the hot bath, but I have to get in and then we have to be on our way," Isabella explained.

"It's not that. It's . . ."

"What is it, Porkita?"

"I don't want to tell you," Porkita answered in a sullen voice.

"Porkita, it's me, Isabella. You know you can tell me anything!"

"Not this."

"What's the matter, Porkita?" Isabella turned toward Grammy, but Grammy just shrugged her shoulders in confusion.

Porkita sighed. "Yes, the water has gotten cold. It's very cold, but I can't come out because . . ." She mumbled the next part.

"I couldn't hear you. You can't come out because of what?"

Another bigger, longer sigh and then tearfully, "Because I'm stuck! I'm stuck in the tub! My hips are lodged in so tight I can't move! The hot water must have made me expand, or maybe it made the tub shrink, but I can't get out!"

Isabella tried not to giggle. She tried really hard, but the giggles bubbled out against her will.

Porkita heard her and yelled, "Oh, wonderful! I am stuck in a pot full of freezing water, and you think it's funny? Sometimes I worry about you, Isabella!"

This made Isabella giggle harder and she wasn't surprised to turn and see Grammy chuckling.

"Here," said Grammy, between chuckles, "hand her this bottle of fruit oil and tell her to pour some in the water. That outta loosen her enough so's we kin pull her out."

Isabella passed the bottle behind the curtain and told Porkita to pour some in and then cover herself with the larger cloth. When she had done so, Grammy and Isabella each took one of her arms and pulled. It took several tugs before the tub released its grip and Porkita popped out.

"Thank you," Porkita said, covering herself with the cloth and trying to act dignified. "That was very kind of you," she said in her most royal voice.

Porkita's formal voice and manner as she stood dripping water and oil onto the floor, having just been sprung from the tub like a cork from a bottle, sent Isabella and Grammy into giggles again. Porkita yanked the curtain closed. Isabella and Grammy could hear her muttering and mumbling as she dressed herself.

When Porkita had put on the clean dress Grammy had laid out for her, she emerged from behind the curtain and sat down at the table. Grammy and Isabella had finally gotten their laughter under control.

"I'm sorry I laughed at you, Porkita. I didn't mean to hurt your feelings," Isabella told her.

Porkita answered, "That's all right, Isabella. I know you couldn't help it." A small smile played across Porkita's lips and she added, "I guess it was kind of funny."

"Best laugh I had in lifetimes," Grammy cackled. Then realizing she might be hurting Porkita's feelings, she added, "'Course, it could've happened to anyone. Must be something wrong with that old tub."

Porkita nodded. "There must be! I have never gotten stuck in my bath at home." Isabella nodded, even as she remembered that Porkita's bath at home was larger than the room they were sitting in.

Isabella helped Grammy scoop the oily water from the metal tub and throw it outside and then refill it with clean water so Isabella could take a quick bath. Once she had finished and had put on the hand-me-down dress from Grammy, she was ready to resume the search for the Lanolions.

As Isabella and Porkita hugged Grammy good-bye, she gave Porkita the quilts and the promised bag of food.

"If yer leavin' jest to protect Orion and me, I wish you would stay," Grammy argued. "We could hide ya and those varmints would never know you were here. If they come round, we could sneak you into the root cellar."

"What's a root cellar?" asked Isabella.

"Thomas built it fer me to keep my fruit and vegetables cool so's they wouldn't rot. It's a hole dug in the earth with a trapdoor on top. Nobody would find it lessen they knowed where to look. You'd be safe there."

"I appreciate you wanting to protect us, Grammy, but what if we couldn't get to the root cellar in time? What if they snuck up on us? And what if we don't find the Lanolions and Rankton does? Then we are all in trouble," explained Isabella.

"It jest seems every time you come to see me, you are in a flousel full of trouble, and I cain't do anything to help ya!" Grammy complained.

"But you have helped me so much!" insisted Isabella. "You took me in and fed me, made me clothes, and cut my tangled hair! This time I showed up with Porkita and you took care of both of us! How can you think you haven't helped me?"

"None of that got you out of trouble and safely home, did it? A twouse thing like you shouldn't be out wanderin' with them ugly soldiers after you! I jest want you to be back home safe with yer parents."

Isabella noticed that instead of joining the conversation, Porkita was helping herself to the food Grammy had packed for their trip.

Gently taking the sack from Porkita, Isabella replied, "I will be, Grammy. I just have to warn the Lanolions. By then, maybe my father's soldiers will find us and take us safely home." She gave the old woman a gentle hug, pet Orion's plumage, and led Porkita out the door.

As they crossed the open meadow in front of Grammy's cabin, Isabella and Porkita turned back to wave at Grammy standing on the porch. Orion circled above them for a short time, and then with a final hoot of farewell, he returned to Grammy's side.

"What are we looking for now, Isabella?" Porkita asked.

"We have to go through a large field of pricker bushes."

"Pricker bushes? You mean bushes with sharp thorns?"

"Yes."

"We'll be scratched to pieces! Can't we go around?" begged Porkita.

"Don't worry, Porkita. We'll be fine. Just follow me closely."

Isabella walked right up to the edge of the vast field of bushes and called, "Hello! Remember me?"

There was no answer.

She tried again. "Yoo-hoo! Can you hear me?"

Nothing.

Porkita leaned in close to Isabella and asked, "Can who hear you? *I* can hear you."

Isabella replied, "Not you. Them."

Porkita thought a minute and then asked, "Who's them?"

"I don't know who they are. Just be patient. Hello! Are you in there?"

There was silence for a few moments as the girls waited and then Porkita asked, "If you don't know who they are, why do you expect them to answer us?"

"Because even though I don't know who they are, I know they're in there."

"Who's *they*? How do you know *they* are in there?" Porkita was getting frustrated.

"I know *they* are in there because they helped guide me through the last time I was here, but I don't know who or what *they* are because I couldn't see them," explained Isabella.

Porkita scratched her head and tried to untangle this riddle, then replied, "Isabella, maybe you couldn't see them because *they* aren't there! There's nothing in these bushes except thorns and prickers!"

Isabella tried one last time. "Hello! Don't you recognize me? I'm the girl you helped when I was stuck in the thorns! I need your help again."

Silence, except for the impatient tapping of Porkita's hoof.

Isabella sighed. "I guess we'll have to find the way through on our own. I wonder where they went? Maybe something scared them away." Isabella began to step into a thorn-free bush, but Porkita's hand on her shoulder stopped her.

"What kind of creature can scare away things that you can't even see?" Porkita whispered in a frightened voice.

"I don't know," answered Isabella. "Just stay close to me."

As Isabella put her foot into the bush, it began to shake violently and Porkita bounded backwards.

"There you are!" Isabella exclaimed. "I was getting worried about you! Can you please help us cross the field?"

There was no response.

"Isabella, what is going on?" Porkita asked in a wavering voice.

"They are just telling us which way is safe," answered Isabella.

"Who is telling us?"

"The things I told you about that you can't see."

Porkita swallowed hard and said, "So there really is something alive in these bushes?"

"Of course. I told you there was."

Isabella stuck her foot into the bush again, and again there was powerful rustling.

"I guess they don't want us to go in here. Let's try another spot." They moved over several feet to another thornless bush, but when Isabella tried to step in, the strong rustling resumed.

"I don't understand," Isabella cried. "Last time they only rustled when there were thorns or danger. I don't see any thorns here, so why are they rustling? Maybe you should try it and see what they do."

"Have you lost your mind?" Porkita hissed. "You want me to stick my foot into a bush that is shaking wildly when we have no idea who or what is making it shake? I don't think so!"

"They won't hurt you, Porkita. They are friendly. They untangled me last time when I was stuck and helped me get safely to the other side of the field. Don't be afraid of them! Just stick your foot in a little ways and see if they shake the bush. It'll be fine, I promise."

Porkita's trust in Isabella was a little greater than her fear of the things in the bushes, so she cautiously stuck first the tip and then all of her hoof into the bush. She yanked it back out when the bush vibrated.

"So what do we do now?" asked Porkita. "There is no way I'm going into these bushes with those *things* rustling like that!"

"I don't know what they are trying to tell us, but they obviously don't want us to enter here. Let's walk along this edge a ways and see if they will let us in further down."

The girls had only taken a few steps when they heard a loud commotion. Isabella pulled Porkita flat onto the ground.

"What is it?" whispered Porkita.

"I don't know," admitted Isabella, also whispering. "You stay down and I'll try to peek over the bushes and see."

"Whatever it is, don't let it see you!" warned Porkita.

"I'll be careful."

Isabella slowly and carefully rose up until she could see over the tops of the bushes. At first she couldn't see anything except branches flying through the air. She could hear the clump of boots and the sound of branches being hacked. Then she saw the glint of the sun as it shone on a large, swinging metal blade and a glimspe of a gruesome face.

Isabella dropped to the ground and grabbed Porkita's arm. "It's Rankton's soldiers! They are cutting their way through the bushes and they're headed right for us! Start crawling along the edge of the bushes as fast as you can!"

The girls scrambled on hands and knees as fast as they could. Isabella kept looking over her shoulder to see how close the soldiers were. She could see the cut branches flying through the air and knew the soldiers were close to breaking through to the open meadow where she and Porkita would be in plain view. When the soldiers were only a few feet from the edge, Isabella became aware that the bushes she was crawling past were gently shaking. She thought she heard a whispery voice say, "Come."

Isabella took a chance. She grabbed Porkita's arm to stop her and then crawled deep into the nearest bush, gesturing for Porkita to follow. They curled up as flat and as small as they could, waiting to be discovered by the soldiers. They could still hear the tramping of the soldiers' boots, but there was no longer the sound of branches being cut. And the boots didn't sound like they were getting closer; they sounded as though they were moving away.

When they could no longer hear any noise at all, Isabella gestured to Porkita to stay still while she crawled to the edge of the brush and peered out. After a moment, she crawled back to Porkita's side.

Keeping her voice low, she said, "I didn't see anything, but that was too close! I think we should stay in the bushes and crawl all the way to the other side just to be safe."

"Do you think they are headed to Grammy's?" asked Porkita. "Do you think Grammy and Orion will be all right?"

"I didn't think about that!" answered Isabella. "I hope they will be all right. Orion will warn Grammy and hopefully she will hide. We could go back to check on them, but I'm afraid it might just make things worse. What do you think we should do?"

"I think we should have a little snack and think about it," suggested Porkita, eyeing the sack of goodies Grammy had packed for them. "I always think better on a full stomach!"

"I'm still full from the breakfast Grammy cooked for us, but you go ahead and help yourself." Porkita dove for the sack and found a corn muffin and a pear to munch on while they talked.

"I hate to leave Grammy alone with those disgusting soldiers!" admitted Isabella.

"Me, too," agreed Porkita, "but think how mad Grammy would be if we went back to see if she was safe and the soldiers caught us."

"Still, I'll be worried sick not knowing if she is safe. What if she needs us? What if those goons hurt her?"

Porkita's pink cheeks went pale, and she dropped the uneaten portion of her muffin. "You're right. We have to go back right away."

"I could go back by myself," offered Isabella. "You could stay hidden here and once I made sure Grammy wasn't in danger, I would come back."

Porkita sat up straight and thrust out her chin defiantly. "We're in this together. Where you go, I go."

"That's very brave of you, Porkita. Thank you."

Porkita's thrust-out chin quivered a bit. "Besides, I don't want to stay here alone with those rustling things."

Isabella smiled and gave her friend a quick hug. "All right, we'll go together. But the rustling things really are friendly! Didn't you hear them tell us to come into the bushes to hide from the soldiers?"

"No, I didn't hear them tell us to do anything."

"Just as the soldiers were getting close enough to see us, the bushes said 'Come' and that's when I motioned for you to follow me in. You didn't hear them?"

"No, Isabella, I didn't hear anything. I just felt you grab my arm and then I saw you go into the bushes."

"And," added Isabella, "that must be why they wouldn't let us in at first! They knew the soldiers were coming, and they were trying to protect us!"

"Well, if that is true, it was nice of them," conceded Porkita, "but," she added, lowering her voice, "they still give me the creeps!" The bushes around her shook in protest.

"Come on, Porkita," Isabella said, taking her friend's hand, "let's go save Grammy!"

Chapter Eleven

Swingin'

The girls crawled out of the bushes, stood, and brushed off their clothes. Holding hands, they headed in the direction of Grammy's house. But before they ventured far, Isabella heard a familiar hoot. Looking up, she saw Orion circling above their heads. The girls stopped and waited as the majestic bird glided down to land gracefully on Isabella's shoulder. Around his neck was a piece of cloth. Isabella untied it and stretched it flat.

On the cloth were the words, "Izabela, I am saf. Orion warnd me abot the soljures and I am hidding in the root seller. Git away from heer fast as you kin. Grammy."

Isabella read the words out loud, then said, "Thank goodness, she's safe! They won't find her in the root cellar."

"Are we still going to go to her, or are we continuing our journey?" asked Porkita.

"I think we should take her advice. Let's head back to the field of thorn bushes."

"Back to the things that rustle? Do we have to? Isn't there any other way?"

"No. We have to try to follow the route I took the first time I passed through here, or we'll never find the Lanolions," explained Isabella.

As soon as they reached the edge of the field, Isabella put one foot into the bushes. There was no rustling, so she continued, holding Porkita's hand and leading her forward. After a few steps, the bush in front of them shook and Isabella smiled as she saw the large thorns protruding from its branches.

"See, Porkita! See how they shake the bush when it has thorns on it! They are helping us," she explained before calling, "Thank you!" to the unseen creatures.

"Yes, thank you," Porkita called, her throat tight with tension. She was careful not to get too close to any bushes that were moving.

157

The princesses slowly made their way through the field avoiding the bushes that shook until they were safely out of the tangle of leaves and thorns.

"We have to be extra careful in this area," Isabella warned. "Not only do we have to avoid Rankton and his men, but it was near here that I met one of those big, hairy beasts for the first time. You know, like the one that injured Lyalus and carried him off to its lair? I remember it chased me through the woods until I hid behind a waterfall and it lost my scent." Isabella thought back to her first journey. "It was not far from here where Malachi, disguised as a talking frog, told me to climb the mountain and look for my home. And right before that, I was at Phinius's hut in the woods. I don't think we will be able to find Phinius's hut because it was pretty well hidden, but we can find the swamp where Phinius pulled me out of the sinking sand."

"Big, hairy beasts, talking frogs, sinking sand-not to mention Rankton and his goons! I'm exhausted just thinking about all of this!" muttered Porkita. "Do you think we could sit down somewhere away from these moving bushes, have something to eat, and talk about what we are doing?"

Isabella led Porkita to a small grove away from the rustling bushes and they sat down to share lunch.

"So we have to get through the sinking sand swamp. Then what?

How are we ever going to find the mountain you fell through? There are mountains everywhere!" complained Porkita.

"I've thought about that, but there weren't that many mountains in that area. Anyway, it was more of a large hill than a mountain. We'll just have to try our best," answered Isabella.

Porkita took another bite of corn muffin and asked, "So, we just have to cross the swamp and the large hill will be on the other side, right?"

"Let me think." Isabella retraced the steps of her original journey in her mind. "No, wait! I forgot about the Gorilmen! We have to go through the tall trees where Argulan and the Gorilmen live. We also have to cross a wide river, but we can swing across on vines. I did that the first time and it wasn't that hard. The river will lead us to a stream and the stream runs right into a cave that is the entrance to the Garden of Robyia! You see, Porkita, we don't have to climb the hill and try to find the hole I fell through. We just have to find the cave I came out of and we can walk right in!"

"Oh, then, that's easy enough!" Porkita replied. "All we have to do is get through a swamp full of sinking sand that can swallow us up, then get past a tribe of half-man, half-monkey people that could swing down from the trees at any time and take us captive, then use a vine to swing across a wide river without drowning, so we can find a hidden cave and save all living creatures! And let's not forget Rankton and his hideous soldiers waiting to ambush us at every turn! Silly me! I don't know what I was worried about! Pass me another corn muffin."

Isabella giggled as she handed her the muffin. "I know it sounds awful, but it isn't as bad as all that! We can make our way safely through the swamp if we just use a stick to poke the ground in front of us. If the stick doesn't sink, neither will we. And the Gorilmen are very nice. They just like to have company to entertain them, that's all. If they grab us, we will just find a way to amuse them, and they will send us on our way."

"Somehow I don't think it will be as easy as you make it sound, but I don't see any other choice, so let's go," Porkita replied.

Isabella chose two strong sticks and they made their way slowly into the swamp, testing the ground before taking each step. Twice they found pools of sinking sand and carefully navigated around them. By the time they reached dry ground, the sun was low in the sky. The forest of tall trees, home of the Gorilmen, stood before them.

"It's up to you, Porkita," Isabella offered, handing her friend some fruit. "Should we camp here for the night and pass through the tall trees in the morning, or should we try to sneak through in the darkness? You decide."

Porkita munched an apple, considered the options and then said,

"More than anything else, I do not want to be captured by the Gorilmen! I know you say they are nice, but I am scared of tall places, scared of being grabbed from behind and swept up to the treetops, and mostly scared that I don't have any talent that they would find remotely entertaining, so I would be stuck there forever!" Porkita's chin wobbled, tears filled her eyes, and she let the half-eaten apple drop to the ground.

Isabella rushed to reassure her. "Porkita! You have lots of talents!"

"Name one."

Isabella was quick to respond, "You are brave! Look how you stood up to the moving rocks and yelled at them. And you are loyal! You have stayed beside me throughout this whole ordeal. And you are smart! You've learned so much on this trip about lighting fires, and cooking, and reading maps! You are the best friend anyone has ever had!"

Porkita eyes were still watery. "Thank you, Isabella. You are very sweet to say all those things. But even if they are true, they're not the kind of talents that would save me from the Gorilmen."

Isabella put her arm around her friend. "You worry too much, Porkita. Let's try to sneak through in the dark, but if the Gorilmen should capture us, I promise I will think of something we can do together to win our release. All right?"

Porkita wiped her nose and eyes with the back of her hand and nodded, then picked up the apple she had dropped. She took a large bite as the two girls set off into the forest.

Isabella led the way. "The Gorilmen probably grab most of their victims off the path," she whispered, "but I don't dare leave the path or we might get lost. We'll just have to move quietly and hope they are too busy dancing and enjoying their party to spot us."

"How do you know they are having a party tonight?" asked Porkita in a hushed voice.

"Because every night is a party to the Gorilmen," answered Isabella. "During the day, they lie around or swing through the trees looking for trespassers, but as soon as it gets dark, they start to play music, dance, and put on shows. They did it every night that I stayed with them." Just then, the girls heard a distant echo of drums. Isabella smiled and said, "It sounds like the party has started. That's good news. We have a better chance of getting through unnoticed. Since the moon is so bright, we will be able to see where we are going, but that also means they will be able to see us clearer."

The deeper into the woods the princesses went, the louder the music grew. When it sounded as though the party was directly overhead, the girls dropped to their knees and crawled. As the sound of music grew fainter, Isabella began to think that they might make it through unnoticed. She stood up, brushing off her hands and knees. Porkita followed suit. Just then, there was a loud *swoosh.* Argulan, the male Gorilmen

162

that had captured Isabella on her last journey, appeared in the path in front of her. Porkita turned to run and slammed squarely into a large hairy chest. She turned back toward Isabella, spitting out several stray Gorilmen hairs.

"So, Princess, you've decided to join our party once again! And this time, you brought a friend! How nice!" Argulan drawled, leaning lazily against the nearest tree trunk.

"Hello, Argulan. How are you?" Isabella greeted him.

"Not a care in the world, Princess, not a care in the world. How about you? Are you still lost, or are you lost once again?"

"Neither one, Argulan. I am retracing the path I took on my first journey. This is my friend, Princess Porkita of the Kingdom of Sowden, and her family was taken hostage. The same evil soldiers who are holding her family captive are trying to catch the two of us. They want me to lead them to the Lanolions. I must reach the land of the Lanolions before these soldiers. I must warn them. I need you to let us pass."

Argulan plucked a twig from a branch and chewed it before responding. "You knew the rules before you entered this part of the forest, Princess. You knew that if you passed through here, you would become our guests until you each shared a talent with us. If you didn't want to visit with us, you shouldn't have come this way." Isabella heard Porkita whimper softly.

"Yes, Argulan, I did know your rules. But I thought you might bend the rules just this one time since it is so important that we reach the Lanolions."

"Reaching these Lanolions is important to you, Princess. Our rules and laws are important to us," explained Argulan, rolling the twig from one corner of his mouth to the other.

"It is important to all of us that I reach the Lanolions before Rankton and his soldiers!" countered Isabella. "If he finds them, he will have complete power over all beings, including the Gorilmen! What good will your rules and laws be then?"

Argulan refused to be swayed. "Our tribe has lived here for many years and has grown strong. That is because we deal with the here and now, not with what might happen. We don't start wars, or desire to have anything that is not already ours; we don't try to change our neighbors, and we don't change our own lives because of what others do. Whatever happens with these soldiers, will happen. It doesn't change the fact that you are trespassing on our land and must pay the price."

"I thought that you would understand how important this is!" Isabella cried. "I thought that once you knew what was at stake, you would let us pass!"

"You thought wrong, Princess," Argulan replied, and Isabella felt a strong pair of arms encircle her waist as she was swung from vine to vine, finally reaching the tree tops. Isabella's feet landed on a wooden platform high in trees and she turned around to watch for Porkita's arrival. She knew how nervous Porkita was about the Gorilmen and wanted to reassure her. She waited several minutes, but Porkita didn't turn up. Argulan came swinging in carrying Isabella's pack and went directly to a pile of fruit to grab a couple of bananas.

Isabella ran to his side. "Argulan! Where is my friend Porkita? Why isn't she here with me? What have you done with her?"

Argulan slowly peeled a banana and ate it in two big bites. "Relax, Princess! Have a banana! You are wound way too tight! The other princess is fine. She'll be here in a minute. Rolamar swung down to grab her, but he couldn't lift your round little friend. He said he swung in, wrapped his arm around her and came to a dead stop. Never happened to him before. So I sent two of my biggest tribe members down to grab her under each arm. It will be tricky since they have to change vines a couple of times to get here, but they should be fine. So just relax, listen to the music, and enjoy yourself."

"I don't want to enjoy myself, Argulan. I want to perform my talent so that you will release me and I can find the Lanolions."

"So, Princess, since you were last here, you have realized that you do have talents. I can't wait to see what you have planned for us!" Argulan grabbed another banana and sauntered over to the where the tribes-

165

people were banging on drums.

Swoosh! Bam! Porkita arrived, supported by a large, hairy Gorilman on either side. Isabella wasn't surprised when Porkita rushed forward and fell into her arms, sobbing.

"Oh, Isabella! It was so awful! It was even more awful than I imagined it would be! First a big hairy goon swung down and just slammed into me! Then two more came and grabbed my arms and we swung and swung! I thought I was going to die! I thought my arms were going to be ripped out of body! And I didn't think we would ever land on solid ground!"

"Hush, Porkita," Isabella soothed, stroking her friend's hair. "You're safe now. Take a deep breath. We need to think about what our talent is going to be so we can get out of here." Isabella led Porkita to an empty spot on the floor and the two girls sat down.

"I can't think about anything when my stomach is growling!" complained Porkita, eyeing the large pile of fruit next to Isabella. Isabella sighed and handed Porkita several bananas and some apples. Porkita bit into one of the apples while she removed the peel from a banana.

"Porkita," asked Isabella, "how can you be scared and crying one minute and feasting the next? I can't even think about eating when I am upset."

Porkita took a moment to swallow the bites of banana that had made her cheeks bulge, then tilted her snout up an inch or two and replied, "Mother says I have a very delicate system. I need to eat frequently, or I feel faint and my mind doesn't work properly. Maybe if you ate something, you would come up with an idea to get us out of here!"

Isabella grabbed an apple from the pile, bit into it with a loud crunch and said, "I'll try anything at this point."

The two girls munched the fruit as they watched the Gorilmen. A number of Gorilmen were making music blowing through long swamp reeds or banging on drums made from skin stretched across hollowed-out gourds. Some were dancing wildly to the music, while others were swinging from the large platform to smaller platforms perched in the trees. There were males, females, and plenty of young Gorilmen joining in the fun. Soon the large platform that held the music-makers was filled with Gorilmen, all talking, laughing, dancing, and enjoying themselves.

"No one is paying any attention to us," Porkita noticed. "Maybe we can escape!"

"Look over the edge. Do you want to try to get down from here on our own?" Isabella asked.

Porkita glanced over the edge, and her pretty pink skin turned green. "No thank you! We will have to find a way to convince them to take us down, and even then, I am keeping my eyes closed the whole way down! Have you thought of anything yet?"

Isabella shook her head. "I'm too tired to think. Let's find somewhere to sleep. Maybe we'll be able to think clearer after we've rested." She took Porkita's hand and pulled her through the crowd of dancers until they reached Argulan.

Argulan continued dancing as he spoke to them. "Are you ready to entertain now, Princess? I will introduce you as soon as the music stops."

"No, Argulan," Isabella said, "we are tired and wish to go to sleep. We'll find a way to entertain your people tomorrow. Is there a place away from the music where we may stay for the night?"

"You got it, Princess. Just let me grab a couple of fellows to haul your friend, and we will be on our way." Argulan danced away.

"To *haul* your friend? What does he mean *haul* your friend?" questioned Porkita. Suddenly she comprehended. "Swinging? Does he mean they are going to swing me from vine to vine again? Absolutely not, Isabella! No more swinging unless they are swinging me to the ground and out of this land!"

"Porkita, be reasonable. The Gorilmen will be playing loud music, stomping their feet, and singing all night long! We have to go to a platform farther away if we are going to get any rest at all!"

Argulan showed up before Porkita could answer. Two of his large hairy friends grabbed Porkita under her arms. As they escorted her to the edge of the platform, Isabella saw her friend go limp, her hooves dragging across the wooden floor. The two males unhooked vines from the trunk of the tree and a moment later they were swinging away into the moonlight.

"Ready, Your Highness?" Argulan asked. At her nod, he wrapped his long arm around her waist and they flew from vine to vine, platform to platform, until they landed on a small platform with several shelters made from branches and leaves. Porkita was lying on the floor in a heap.

Isabella rushed to her side. "What happened? What did you do to her?"

"Nothing," answered one of the large Gorilmen. "As soon as we took hold of her, she collapsed! I thought it was bad when she was kicking and screaming, but she is twice as heavy like this!" Before swinging away, he told Argulan, "Get someone else to move her next time!"

Porkita regained consciousness and Isabella helped her stumbling friend into a shelter. Porkita fell gratefully onto one of the leafy mats and went right to sleep.

"Everything all right?" Argulan asked. At Isabella's nod, he said, "I'll leave you then. See you tomorrow, Princess."

Isabella checked to make sure Porkita was okay, then collapsed on the other mat and slept deeply.

The sun was high when the girls walked out of the shelter the next day, yet most of the tribe was still asleep. There was a pile of freshly picked fruit and a gourd of water sitting in front of their hut, and Isabella assumed Argulan had put it there for their breakfast. They sat in the center of the platform, splashes of sunlight warming their skin through the ceiling of leaves.

"It was nice of Argulan to leave fruit for us," observed Porkita, "but what I wouldn't give for some corn casserole! Or a lovely corn pudding! Anything hot and made with corn would taste wonderful after eating just fruit!"

"I think there are some of Grammy's corn muffins left in my pack, but Argulan has it."

"No, he doesn't," Porkita insisted. "I saw it on the floor of the shelter this morning. He must have left it when he left the fruit."

Isabella went into the shelter and came out again bearing her pack. "How would you like a nice corn muffin to go with your apples and bananas? It isn't hot, but it *is* made of corn."

As they finished eating, Porkita asked, "Are you sure there isn't any way for us to get down from here on our own? Can't we just slide straight down one of these vines?"

"Not all of them reach the ground and then we would be stranded. Plus, Argulan and his friends would come after us. The only way out is to pay their toll and entertain them. But what can we do?"

"I can read! I've learned to read quite a few words since Father said we could have lessons!"

"I can read, too, but what would we read to them? We don't have any books," Isabella reminded her.

"Well, that's all I've learned. I didn't have time to learn to sing or dance or anything."

"Me, neither. I know there is something we can do. We just have to think of something. Last time, they let me go because I made them laugh when I shot water out of my mouth. So it doesn't have to be singing or dancing; it can just be something they haven't seen before. That's why they want visitors, because they're bored."

"Well, we both are anxious to get out of here, but I have to admit I am enjoying the constant supply of free food, and I really liked the dancing last night. The way they move together and the gestures they make; it's almost as though they are telling a story with their movements."

"That's it!" cried Isabella. "That's what we can do for our talent!"

Chapter Twelve

Hamming It Up

"I could tell one of the stories Phinius told me! I'm sure that would win our release," said Isabella.

"But what about me? Don't I have to do something, too?"

"You could act out the story while I tell it!"

Porkita frowned. "I don't know anything about acting. What would I do?"

"We'll figure something out. We can work on it all day and perform it tonight. That way we can be on our way tonight or first thing tomorrow morning. What do you think?" suggested Isabella.

"I think you are crazy to want me to act. I think they are going to laugh at us and hold us captive forever. But since I don't have a better idea, let's try it."

Finding a secluded spot on the platform, Isabella told Porkita several of Phinius's stories and they chose the one they thought would work best. They had just started planning Porkita's movements when Argulan swung in.

"Good morning, Princesses!" Argulan called, even though it was obvious from the position of the sun that it was past lunchtime. "Were you able to get any rest?"

"Yes, thank you, Argulan," Isabella replied.

"I came to collect you and take you to the main platform. Most of my tribe gathers there during the daylight hours. You are welcome to join us."

"No, thank you. We'll be fine here. We have plenty to eat, and we are busy working on a surprise for the tribe."

Argulan's eyes lit up. "What is it?"

Isabella answered, "It's a surprise, Argulan. You have to leave us alone so we can finish."

"Very well, Princess. I can't wait until this evening's celebration! I will come back for you when the festivities begin. Only I hope you remember that you won't be released unless the tribe approves of your performance." On that note, Argulan grabbed a vine and disappeared into the trees.

Porkita tried to act out the story as Isabella told it, but she wasn't familiar with the creatures from Phinius's tale. She didn't know how they should move or what sounds they would make. As dusk approached, she grew more and more frustrated.

"I can't do this, Isabella! I just can't," Porkita insisted, sinking to the ground and wiping the sweat from her brow. Isabella knelt down beside her.

"Do you want to tell the story and I'll act it out?" offered Isabella.

"I will never remember it, especially with all those Gorilmen staring at me. Besides, you tell it so well in that scary voice."

"Then you'll just have to do the acting. You are doing fine, Porkita. Just keep trying."

"Why couldn't Phinius have written a story about things I know? If it was a story about the way people in the royal court act, I could do it. Or if he wrote about a royal feast, I would be perfect. But he had to write stories about finargles and pelatries! I have never even heard of them, much less seen any!"

"Porkita!" Isabella yelled, jumping to her feet. "You're a genius!"

"I am? Why?"

"You said the story should be about something you know! What do you know better than what you have been living through for the past couple of weeks? We'll tell the Gorilmen about our capture by Rankton, and you can act it out!"

Porkita thought a moment. "I guess I could do that. Let's practice and see how it goes."

The sound of drums broke the stillness of the day, as Argulan and two of his tribesmen came swinging through the shadows to land next to the girls.

"It's show time, Princesses! I told the tribe that you have been working on something special all day and they are so eager to see it, they have started the party earlier than usual!" Argulan told them.

"We need a little more time, Argulan, so we can make it perfect," said Isabella, seeing the panicked look on Porkita's face.

"Can't do it, Princess. The rule is that when the drums sound, the show begins. You are the main attraction tonight, so you are first."

Before Isabella could protest further, she heard a strangled cry of "I-s-a-bella!" and saw Porkita being carried off by the two burly tribesmen. Argulan handed Isabella her pack, then wrapped his arm around her waist and off they flew into the night.

To Isabella, there seemed to be even more tribes-people on the large platform than there were last night. She could barely squeeze through the crowd to find Porkita, who had been led to a spot next to the drums. As soon as she joined Porkita, her friend grabbed her arm and started shaking it.

"Isabella, what are we going to do? We haven't even practiced this!"

"Don't panic, Porkita; we'll just do it and if it doesn't win their approval, we'll try something else tomorrow. Just listen as I tell the story and act out what I say, all right?"

"We're going to be awful! What if they throw fruit at us or something?"

"Actually, throwing fruit at us might mean they like it! The worst thing would be if they just sat there staring at us without any reaction at all. We should really try—"

"My fellow Gorilmen," Argulan's strong voice interrupted her. "It is a great honor to introduce tonight's presentation for your amusement. Returning to entertain us for a second time is Princess Isabella of Grom! Princess Isabella is the one who taught us that lovely water-spitting game that we all enjoy so much." There were cheers and lots of foot-stomping. "Also joining us tonight is another princess. Here for the first time is Princess Porkita of---where are you from, Princess?"

Porkita mumbled, "Sowden. The Kingdom of Sowden."

Argulan bowed and continued, "Princess Porkita of the Kingdom of Sowden! Please welcome our guests." Most of the spectators cheered politely.

"You can begin, Princesses," invited Argulan, taking a seat on the floor at the front of the crowd.

Isabella took a deep breath, set down her pack, smiled encouraging at Porkita, and began.

"A wedding was planned. Guests were coming from all over the land to witness the wedding of Princess Hogitha and Prince Hogden. Feasts were prepared and the palace was bustling with excitement." Isabella heard a few impatient murmurs from the audience. She glanced at Porkita and saw that she was standing frozen like a statue.

Isabella slammed her hand down hard on the nearest drum, startling the crowd and bringing Porkita out of her trance.

"Bam! Suddenly the joyous celebration turned into a nightmare! A group of hideous soldiers entered the castle and took the royal family hostage! These soldiers were so grotesque that it was hard to look at them! Their backs were hunched, their eyes were crossed, and they had long, sharp teeth! Show them what they looked like, Porkita!"

At Porkita's blank stare, Isabella whispered, "Hunch your back, cross your eyes, and bare your teeth!" Porkita hunched her back a bit, crossed her eyes, and pulled back her lips, but ended up with a goofy smile instead of a fear-inducing grimace. A few chuckles came from the crowd.

"The leader of the soldiers was named Rankton, and he was the most vicious creature alive! He was tall with small beady eyes, and he liked to strut around knocking others out of his way." Porkita strutted in front of the audience, her shoulders thrown back, and pretended to push creatures out of the way, but only succeeded in knocking over several drums.

"Rankton tied up the royal family." Porkita crossed her wrists as though they were tied. "He discovered that two members of the royalty were missing, and they were the two he needed the most! He was very angry!" Porkita pretended to search and then throw a temper tantrum. The Gorilmen were warming up to the story and began to laugh openly at Porkita's antics.

"The two princesses he sought had escaped! But he followed them and captured them. He wanted them to lead him to something very valuable. The princesses pretended to show him the way, but it was a trick. Instead, they led him to a field of rocks. They told him the rocks would take him where he wanted to go. But he kicked one and it bit his foot!" Porkita acted out the whole scene, ending with Rankton hopping on one foot, shaking his fist in the air. The Gorilmen started slapping each other on the back. Some even rose to try hopping on one foot themselves.

"Then the princesses tricked him into entering a swamp full of frogs that spit poison. This poison burns the skin. The princesses put on their magic cloaks and were safe, but Rankton and his evil soldiers were covered in frog spit and burns."

Porkita looked around wildly, then grabbed an orange from a member of the audience. She bit a hole in it, then squeezed it so the juice shot out and hit her in the face, just as the frog spit had. She clutched her face, then rolled on the floor and wailed as though she was dying.

The Gorilmen scrambled to find oranges for themselves and shot the juice at one another, falling and rolling on the ground in pretend agony. Soon their fur was covered in the sticky mess. Isabella continued, yelling to be heard over the chaos, inventing things to make it more exciting for the Gorilmen.

"The evil Rankton was very angry and more determined than ever to find the hidden treasure so he could rule the land! The princesses were running out of ways to trick him. They decided to lead him into the lair of the dreaded beast! The beast was even taller than Rankton, with huge paws and the strength of ten Gorilmen. But Rankton stood up to the beast, slicing at him with his blade." Porkita seized a banana to use as the blade and sliced it through the air and into the imaginary beast. Immediately, the Gorilmen all had bananas in their hands and were doing battle with each other. Since the bananas were ripe, the skins soon split and pieces of banana flew everywhere. Porkita joined the fun, pretending to fight off Gorilmen after Gorilmen with her trusty banana. Isabella just watched, but had to duck out of the way of the occasional flying banana piece or peel.

Argulan came over, banana in hand and bowed to Isabella. "You have done it again, Princess. You have brought laughter and joy to my tribe. I don't think they are going to settle down enough to hear any more of your tale, though. Would you like to stay the night, or would you like me to take you to the forest floor so you can be on your way?"

"I am glad your tribe enjoyed the story, Argulan. Let me get Porkita, and we will be ready to leave." Isabella pushed her way through the feuding fruit wielders and embraced her friend. "Porkita, you were wonderful! And we did it; we are free to go! Argulan said they will take us down to the forest floor right away! Come on!"

"This was so much fun, Isabella! I think I like the Gorilmen's rule. I think everyone who travels to our palace should have to put on a show for us! Wouldn't that be wonderful?" Porkita did a little dance as she carved letters in the air with her banana.

"Yes, Porkita, that would be wonderful," answered Isabella. "But it is time to leave now, so let's go!"

"You want to know a secret, Isabella?" Porkita asked as they made their way to Argulan. "I was so afraid of being captured by the Goril-men, but I ended up having the best time! I love all the delicious fruit, the music and dancing, and tonight was the most fun of all! I'm not even going to close my eyes when they take us down! I'm going to pretend I am flying!"

After the princesses waved goodbye to all of the Gorilmen, Argulan and two of his tribesmen took them safely to the ground, Porkita screaming, "Wheeee!" the whole way.

"Goodbye again, Princess. I hope your journey will have the results you desire," said Argulan, bowing to her. "But remember, sometimes it is better to worry less about what is happening in the lands out there," he told her, gesturing outside the forest, "and to concentrate on making those in your own little land happy. That is what has worked for the Gorilmen for a very long time. Good-bye to you, too, Princess Porkita. Safe journey!" And with a running jump, he and his tribesmen swung from vine to vine to return to their home among the treetops.

Porkita and Isabella managed to find their way out of the dark forest and set up camp for the night. As they lay in the moonlight on Grammy's quilts, Isabella noticed that Porkita was smiling strangely.

"What are you thinking about?" she asked.

Porkita grinned and answered, "I was just picturing my father's face when I tell him I want to learn to be an actress."

Isabella woke the next morning with a flutter of excitement in her stomach. She shook Porkita awake and took some fruit from her pack for their breakfast.

Porkita looked at her groggily. "No fire? No hot breakfast?"

"Not this morning. We are so close. I can feel it. I'm anxious to get on our way. Besides, we have no idea how close Rankton is and the smoke from the fire might lead him to us."

After gobbling the fruit, they packed up the quilts and began.

"Now we just have to continue in this direction," Isabella said, "and we should come to the big river. A river that wide would be hard to miss!"

The girls spent the better part of the morning hiking across the wilderness, fighting their way through thick brush and scrambling over small hills. By the time they stopped for a midday meal, they were exhausted.

"Isabella, are you sure the river is this way? Maybe we made a wrong turn somewhere!"

"We didn't make any turns, Porkita! It has to be somewhere in front of us. I just know it!"

"Well, I'm too tired to wander around all day looking for the river!" whined Porkita. "Can't we rest here until the sun goes down a little? It is so hot it feels like my skin is sizzling!"

"How about if we rest here for a few more minutes and then try again? Just concentrate on how lovely the cool waters of the river will feel on your sizzling skin!"

When Isabella finally convinced her friend to continue, they moved through the thicket single file, Isabella trying to forge a path for Porkita. Just as the sun dropped low enough so that its rays no longer burned their skin, Isabella stopped abruptly.

"What is it?" Porkita hissed.

"Listen!"

"What is it? I don't hear anything!"

"Listen harder!" Isabella insisted. Then Porkita heard it, too. It was the sound of water rushing past.

"Do you think it's the river?" asked Porkita. "Did we find it?"

"It has to be. We're almost there, Porkita!" Isabella pushed her way through the tangle of bushes toward the sound, Porkita following a few yards behind. Suddenly, Isabella disappeared into thin air.

Porkita froze in her tracks. "Isabella? Where are you?"

She heard a muffled voice call, "Down here, Porkita. Be careful you don't fall in, too."

Porkita cautiously moved closer and saw a hole in the ground hidden among the bushes. Peering in, she could just see the very top of Isabella's head.

"Isabella! Are you hurt?" she cried.

"No, I don't think so. A few scratches, maybe, but nothing serious."

"Are you stuck? Should I pull you out by your hair?" asked Porkita.

"No! Don't pull my hair! Thank you for offering, but I think I can turn over and crawl out on my own."

Porkita watched as the patch of golden hair began to rotate. Then, halfway around, it stopped.

"Something furry just brushed my foot!" Isabella screamed. "What is that noise? Something is sniffing me! There's a rope or something wrapped around my leg! And my other leg—aaaahhhhh!" Before Porkita could react, Isabella was gone.

"Isabella!" Porkita screamed. "Where are you? Isabella! What should I do?" She knelt down and stuck her head in the hole, but there was no sign of her friend.

Chapter Thirteen

Beneath the Earth

Feeling as though her legs were being torn from her body, Isabella was dragged deeper and deeper into the darkness of the tunnel. She ran her hands along the walls, hoping to grab onto something that would help her resist, but only succeeded in scraping flesh from her dirtied hands. Rocks and roots dug into her back and legs as she bounced helplessly along, loose dirt pelting her face. A strong combination of odors burned Isabella's nostrils and made her eyes water: the earthy scent of freshly turned soil, the acrid smell of rotting plants, and the unmistakable stench of animal waste. Finally, the tension on her legs eased as they slowed and then stopped.

Isabella felt the whip-like cords that were binding her legs loosen. She rolled over onto her hands and knees, wincing in pain, and began to feel around in the darkness. All around her she could hear sniffing and scratching. She tried to crawl forward, but bumped her head several times on the low ceiling. Running her hands along the ceiling and floor, she determined that she was no longer in a tunnel, but in a large opening. As she swept her hand along the floor, she could hear creatures scurrying out of the way. Occasionally, her hand would encounter a pile of something warm and mushy, but she forced herself not to think about what it could be.

She followed the curve of the ceiling with her hand, letting it guide her to the nearest wall. Feeling her way along the wall until she reached an opening, she was kept from escaping by a large furry snout pushing at her hand. Isabella quickly scooted away from the creature, only to feel another pointy nose dig into her back. No matter which direction she moved in, there was another large creature blocking her path. Heart pounding, Isabella sucked air into her starved lungs in noisy gulps. There wasn't even a hint of light to guide her. She listened to the squeaking and sniffing noises. They were coming from all sides. She was surrounded by the creatures without any hope of escaping.

Isabella felt the first set of teeth as they tore into the flesh on her shin. She kicked her leg and heard the creature squeal as it hit the dirt wall. Instantly, many more creatures attacked her. She punched, kicked, swatted, and slapped, her screams echoing through the tunnels. She tried rolling back and forth across the floor, reasoning that a moving target would be harder to find in the darkness, but still they pounced on her.

Isabella was growing exhausted from the battle. Her struggles weakened as the creatures' assaults strengthened. She gave only a few feeble kicks and a last shaky scream as the creatures covered her from head to toe.

A flicker of light in the inky blackness caught Isabella's weary eye. Sure she had imagined it, she was shocked to see more flashes of light. Then a voice called, "Hang on, Isabella! I'm coming!" Porkita's voice gave Isabella the inspiration she needed to begin fighting off the creatures once more. Knocking them away with her bloodied arms and legs, she dragged herself toward the light. Before she reached it, the light grew much stronger. A flaming torch burst out of one of the holes, held up by a pudgy pink arm. The creatures reacted immediately, screeching as if in agony and abandoning their attack on Isabella to seek the corners untouched by the light.

The rest of Porkita followed the torch, her clothes torn and her skin dirtied. "Isabella! Are you all right?" she panted. "I came as fast as I could, but I made a couple of wrong turns."

Isabella threw herself into her best friend's arms and sobbed. The light from the torch was strong enough for Porkita to see the blood running from Isabella's wounds.

"Oh, Isabella! You're hurt bad! We have to get you out of here. Can you crawl?"

Isabella continued to sob, but nodded. "They are still here. Whatever they are, they are still here with us."

"Where?" asked Porkita, looking around the area.

Isabella took the torch from her hands and stabbed it toward the darkness. The creatures squealed and scrambled over each other in their need to avoid the light, but Isabella and Porkita caught a glimpse of them for the first time and were horrified by what they saw. Covered in coarse brown fur, the animals were as long as Isabella's arm, with stubby legs that kept their fat bodies close to the ground. The light shone off their enormous eyes and the sharp teeth that had feasted on Isabella. Whipping behind them was a cord-like tail that Isabella was sure they had wrapped around her legs to drag her to their den. Both girls shuddered at the blood dripping from the animals' teeth and fur-Isabella's blood.

"Come on!" Porkita urged. "Let's get out of here." She took the torch and started toward the opening. Almost immediately, the creatures used the return of darkness to resume their attack on Isabella.

"Porkita!" Isabella screamed, pain and terror overwhelming her. As Porkita turned back with the torch, the creatures ran.

"You can't take the light!" Isabella wailed. "We need to keep the light behind us so they don't attack. They are afraid of the light or maybe it hurts them somehow."

"But how can we keep the light behind us? Should I rip off a piece of my slip and tie the torch to my ankle so it drags behind me?"

"I'm afraid if it drags in the dirt, it will go out, and then we won't have any defense against them."

"So what do we do?" asked Porkita.

"I guess—I guess one of us will have to crawl backwards and wave the torch at anything that tries to follow."

Porkita listened to the noises coming from the darkness, looked at Isabella's wounds, and shuddered, but she still said, "I'll do it, Isabella. You are injured. You go on ahead, and I'll make sure none of them get close to you again."

Isabella stared at her friend, amazed at her sudden courage. This Porkita was a far cry from the frightened, fragile princess who began the journey with Isabella. "Thank you, Porkita," was all that she could manage around the lump in her throat.

Isabella started toward the opening, but Porkita stopped her. "Wait,

Isabella. They might come from that direction. I wrapped some of my slip around a couple of branches to make the torch. Let me see if I can break some off and give it to you so you can light the tunnel in front of you. That way you'll be able to see where you are going and also scare off any creatures that come at you." As she pulled the branches apart, the lit fabric dropped to the ground.

"Quick, rip off another piece of your slip and wrap it around your branches!" directed Isabella, as she did the same to the branches Porkita had given her. Then they were both able to light their separate torches from the burning material on the ground. "Maybe leaving this fire on the ground will keep them from following us right away."

Isabella went first, dirt, animal waste and stones imbedding into her open sores with each painful movement. She waved the torch back and forth in front of her, making sure nothing blocked her path. Porkita backed into the tunnel behind her, careful not to bump Isabella's injured legs. Their progress was slow, because of Isabella's wounds and because it took time to find their way out of the intricate maze of tunnels. But at long last, they made it out.

Isabella threw herself over the edge of the opening into the evening shadows and crawled toward the sound of the river, Porkita quickly joining her. After a torturous struggle through the brush, they reached the bank of the river at last. Isabella immediately dropped her torch and lowered her body into the cool, rushing water, clinging to thick tree roots to keep from being swept away by the current. Tears streamed down her face as the river tore at the dirt and stones in her wounds and loosened them. Porkita sat nearby, watching her friend's agony and feeling helpless. Isabella finished by dipping her head under the water to wash away the blood clotted in her hair, then dragged herself, shivering, onto the bank.

"What can I do for you, Isabella? Can I do anything to help?" Porkita's heart ached for her friend.

"Do we still have Grammy's pack?" Isabella asked through teeth gritted against the pain.

"I'll find it!" promised Porkita. "I left it where you dropped it when you fell in the hole. I'm sure I can find it as long as I have the torch."

Isabella sat, shaking with cold and pain, for many minutes until she heard Porkita cry, "I found it! I'm coming, Isabella!"

Porkita pushed her way through the bushes. Isabella took the bundle, untied it, and dug until she found the bar of homemade soap Grammy had packed. She also found some soft squares of cloth Grammy had stuck in for washing themselves.

"Can you wet this cloth for me, Porkita?"

Porkita did as she asked. Isabella rubbed soap all over the wet cloth, then began to slowly, excruciatingly clean the bite-marks and scratches on her body. She had to ask Porkita to rinse the cloth several times since it quickly became covered in blood and grime.

Isabella laid her hand on her friend's arm. "I need you to do something for me. It won't be easy and it might upset you, but I need you to do it anyway."

"Whatever you need, Isabella, you only have to ask. What do you need?"

"There are two places that I know of where stones are stuck into my cuts. I need you to dig them out for me."

Porkita's normally pink skin turned slightly green. "Dig them out? I can't, Isabella. I can't bear to hurt you like that!"

"You have to, Porkita. It will hurt, yes, but if you don't it will get worse, and I will get very ill. Phinius taught me all about how important it is to keep wounds clean. I would try to do it myself, but I can't reach them. One is on the back of my leg and the other is on my shoulder. I can feel the stones, but I can't get them out." Porkita still had a horrified expression on her face, so Isabella begged. "Please, Porkita, please! I know it is unpleasant, but it has to be done. Just find a stick with a sharp point and loosen the stones from my skin. I'll hold the torch so you can see what you're doing. Once the stones are out, we can find a place to rest for the night."

Porkita slowly rose and searched the bushes along the river's bank for a stick that would serve her purposes. She found one that was fairly sharp and Isabella showed her how to rub it against a rock to sharpen it even more. Once it had a nice point on it, Isabella turned and showed Porkita the spot on her shoulder that needed attention.

"Can you see all right? Do you need me to hold the torch higher?" Isabella asked.

"No, the torch is fine."

Isabella tensed and waited, but nothing touched her skin.

"Porkita?"

"I don't think I can do this, Isabella. I want to help you, but I think I am going to be sick just thinking about . . ."

"Porkita! Listen to me! You can do this! Look at all the things you have done since we left your kingdom that you never thought you could do! Why, you made a torch and crawled into that hole to save me from those creatures and you didn't have any idea what was waiting in there! If you can do that, this will be easy. Just take deep breaths and do it! I might cry out, but don't stop no matter what!" Isabella instructed.

"All right, Isabella, I will try. Do you want something to bite down on for the pain? My father once had a splinter of wood caught in his hoof and the medical adviser gave him a knotted cloth to bite on while he removed it. I could rip off a piece of my dress . . . no, that's too dirty to put in your mouth. I could give you a piece of Grammy's fruit or an

193

ear of corn! That would work!"

Isabella gave her friend a weak smile. "No, thank you, Porkita. I'll be fine. Just get it over with, please."

Isabella heard Porkita take several deep breaths, then cried out as she felt the sharp stick enter her wound. Porkita fumbled a couple of times before calling, "I got it! It's out, Isabella!" Isabella slumped forward in pain.

"Are you all right? I'm sorry it took me so long. I'm not very good at this," Porkita admitted, her voice shaky.

"You did fine," Isabella answered in a voice heavy with exhaustion and pain. "Now let's do the other one and get it over with so we can get some sleep." She turned onto her stomach and showed Porkita the other wound.

"Oh, Isabella! This stone is even bigger. Are you ready?"

Isabella nodded wearily. Porkita took a deep breath, stuck the stick in, and removed the stone with one quick movement. Blood gushed from the open cut, but the stone was out.

"Can you clean it for me?" asked Isabella, handing Porkita the soapy cloth. Porkita managed to wipe the cut several times before diving into the bushes to vomit.

"Are you all right?" Isabella asked from where she still lay on the ground.

"M-m-m. I'll be fine," Porkita answered as she came back to the river's edge to rinse her hands, face, and mouth. "Do you need anything else? Please don't need anything else!"

"There is a plant that contains a medicine that would help with the pain and healing, but it's too dark, and we're too tired to find it tonight. Let's find somewhere to sleep and we'll look for it in the morning."

"Can't we just sleep here?" asked Porkita, exhaustion catching up with her.

"No, too many animals come to the river's edge to drink at night. We wouldn't be safe. Let's just crawl back into the bushes a way."

"What about those creatures? What if they come out of their holes at night and attack us?" a fearful Porkita asked.

"You're right, Porkita. Where can we go to be safe?" The girls looked around.

"How about that tree?" asked Isabella. The large tree trunk she pointed at was hollow and had fallen across two smaller trees, which supported it several feet off the ground. The princesses went to investigate and found that there was plenty of room for them to crawl inside and sleep.

"We can even stick our torches in these knotholes so they will burn for a little while longer and protect us from those awful things!" Porkita suggested.

"Great idea, Porkita," said Isabella. They laid their quilts in the hollow of the trunk and climbed in on top of them. Sticking the torches safely in two holes, the girls pulled the quilts around their bodies and settled in for the night. Isabella tossed and turned, her pain slightly greater than her exhaustion.

"Isabella?" Porkita murmured, her voice low and sleepy.

"Yes?"

"Are you going to be all right?"

"I think so. Once I find a side of my body that doesn't hurt to lie on, I should be able to sleep."

Then, "Isabella?"

"Yes, Porkita?"

"You know how you said I was brave to come into the hole to save you?"

"Yes."

"I wasn't brave. I was just more afraid to be left out here alone than I was of what might be in the hole!"

"You were afraid, but you came in to save me anyway. That's what being brave is, Porkita. I'm proud of you," Isabella told her, her words slurring from fatigue.

"Thank you, Isabella," Porkita said, stifling a big yawn. "Good night! Wake me if you need me."

Chapter Fourteen

Whiskers and Venison

Porkita woke before the sun had fully risen. A frightening sound had disturbed her sleep. She turned to wake Isabella and ask what the sound was, but froze. Isabella was *making* the strange moaning sound.

"Isabella! What are you doing? You woke me up with all that noise!"

Isabella's head twisted from side to side as she answered, "I don't feel well, Porkita. I think I'm sick."

"What kind of sick?"

"I don't know," Isabella answered, her voice ragged and her body shaking violently. "One minute I'm cold, and then I'm hot. My whole body hurts, especially my head, which is strange because they didn't bite me on my head. It feels like the Gorilmen are pounding out a beat on my skull." A tear slipped from the corner of Isabella's eye. "I want my mother," she sobbed.

Porkita swallowed hard. "What do you want me to do?"

"Can I have a drink of water? My throat is dry."

"Of course. Right away." Porkita lowered herself from the tree trunk and headed to the river. A moment later, she was back. "What should I put the water in, Isabella?"

Isabella's voice was weak as she replied, "A gourd. Put it in a gourd."

Porkita left only to return once again. "Where would I find a gourd, Isabella?"

"Isn't there one in the pack?"

Porkita climbed back into the tree trunk and saying, "Excuse me, excuse me," she clambered over Isabella's battered body to reach the pack. "The gourds in here already have water in them. Do you want that?"

"No. Can you empty one out and fill it with fresh water from the river?"

"Of course." Porkita scrambled back over Isabella, sloshing water from the gourd onto her and causing her moans to grow louder, then dropped to the ground. She left Isabella in peace for a moment and Isabella dozed. She was rudely awakened by Porkita climbing over her body once more.

"Porkita!" Isabella groaned. "What are you doing now? Did you get me the water?"

"I tried, Isabella, but the current is so strong it ripped the gourd right out of my hands and washed it away before I could catch it! I'm getting the other one now. You'll have a nice drink of fresh water before you know it!"

"Be careful. That is our last gourd. Be sure you don't . . ." Porkita waited for a moment, but Isabella's voice faded away.

"Isabella?"

Isabella jerked, then answered, "What?"

"You were saying?"

"I was saying what?" the weary voice asked.

"I said I was going to get water in the other gourd, and you said be careful, be sure you don't . . . And then you didn't say what I should be careful of."

Silence. Porkita shook her shoulder and called, "Isabella!"

A startled, "What?"

"What should I be careful of?" asked a worried Porkita.

"You should always . . . never forget . . . be careful when you cross the swamp, because . . . you never know how long you will have to . . . kick the frogs and they will move," came the jumbled reply.

"Isabella, I am going to get you some water now because I think you really need it! There isn't any swamp and there aren't any frogs. Just a river full of water and a gourd that needs filling. I'll be right back." Porkita made her way to the river once again.

When she returned, Isabella was asleep again, but Porkita gently lifted her friend's head and poured water onto her still lips. The cool water awakened Isabella and she swallowed several sips. Porkita was alarmed by the heat radiating from Isabella's head and body.

"Isabella? What else can I do? Your body is so hot! Do you want to bathe in the river to cool off?"

"I am not hot! I am freezing! Can you wrap my quilt around me tighter?" Porkita did as she asked, then grabbed her own quilt and added it to the pile, but still Isabella shook with cold.

As the sun rose, Porkita helped herself to several pieces of corn and an apple from their depleting supplies. She watched helplessly as Isabella moaned, tossed, and shivered. Morning passed into afternoon and still Isabella slept.

Abruptly, Isabella threw the quilts from her body and sat up, startling Porkita. She crawled past Porkita and plunged out of the trunk to the ground. As Porkita watched, Isabella stumbled toward the river, ripping the gown from her body. Porkita jumped down and followed, calling to her friend to wait. Isabella's gown dropped to the ground and Porkita scooped it up. She caught up to Isabella just as she was about to plunge into the raging cold water.

Isabella was mumbling, "You'll never take me alive! I have the key to the gate and a brand new gown!"

Porkita grabbed her by her shoulders and pulled her safely back away from the river's bank. Isabella fought her, yelling, "Let me go! I must free the children from the corn! They can't hear the music unless I save them and take them to the frogs!" Porkita firmly guided Isabella to a sitting position on the hard ground and held her there. Isabella struggled for a moment more, and then all the fight seemed to drain out of her.

Porkita slipped the gown over Isabella's head and as she did so, she noticed that Isabella's sores were deep red and angry-looking.

"Isabella, your wounds look worse than they did last night, especially the one on your shoulder where I removed the stone. Do you think we should wash them again?" There was no answer. Porkita tilted up Isabella's chin to look into her eyes. Isabella's eyes were bright, shiny, and totally unfocused.

"Isabella! Isabella!" Porkita cried, terrified by her friend's condition.

"Answer me! Do you know who I am? It's me, Porkita! Isabella, you have to know who I am!"

Isabella replied, "My father will send soldiers to free me from you! More soldiers than the trees in the forest! Then, together, my father and I will battle the beast and make a feast of venison and . . . whiskers."

Porkita drew her sick friend into her arms and rocked back and forth, wailing at her own helplessness. Isabella allowed herself to be held as all of Porkita's fatigue, frustration, and feelings of vulnerability fueled her cries. Once she was spent, Porkita hiccupped several times and tried to figure out what to do next. Her only guide was the way Isabella had taken care of her after the spitting-frog incident.

So she straightened her spine, thrust out her snout, and said in an only slightly quavering voice, "Don't worry, Isabella. I'm going to take care of you. You are going to be fine."

She pulled Isabella to her feet, supporting her as she led her to the area near the fallen tree trunk. Porkita pulled out one of the quilts and helped Isabella to lay on it. Then she wrapped the other quilt around her friend. Isabella lay humming strange melodies to herself. Porkita gathered stray branches into a pile, plopped a large rock in the center and started the branches on fire. Once the fire was burning strongly, she put the gourd full of water onto the rock and waited for it to heat. When the water became hot, Porkita used two sticks to remove the gourd, spilling only a little in the process. She dipped one of the cloths into the hot water, rubbed soap all over it, and proceeded to bathe Isabella's wounds, giving special attention to the one on her shoulder.

Porkita did a thorough job, despite Isabella's moans of pain. Once Isabella had been cleansed, Porkita covered her back up with the quilt. She rinsed out the gourd in the river, being careful not to let it wash away. She left a little water in the bottom, carried it back to the campsite and placed it on the fire. Smashing two apples with a small rock, she placed the pieces into the gourd and let the whole mixture stew. When it was cooked, she took it off and looked at it. It didn't look like the apple stew Isabella had made for her. There were seeds, stems, and large chunks of apple in it, but Porkita reasoned it was better than nothing, so using a leaf, she spooned several bites into Isabella's mouth.

Porkita sat up all night, guarding the campsite, mopping Isabella's hot brow, and coaxing her friend to take an occasional sip of water or bite of food. No matter how loudly her own stomach growled, Porkita did not take one bite of the apple stew. She saved it all for Isabella.

As the sun rose, Porkita heated water and bathed Isabella's wounds again, noticing that they didn't seem as red this time. When she finished, she snuggled in next to her friend and both girls slept deeply.

Porkita woke up and quickly checked to make sure Isabella hadn't wandered off. She was relieved to find her friend still sleeping peacefully. She added fresh branches to the coals of the fire and put water on to heat so she could bath Isabella again.

"Porkita." A raspy voice called to her.

"Isabella! You know who I am! I'm so glad!" Porkita rushed to gently hug her.

"Of course I know who you are, Porkita," she rasped. "May I have a drink of water, please?"

"Of course." Porkita rushed to grab the gourd from the fire and burned herself. She dropped the hot gourd and the water from it doused part of the fire.

"I'll be there in just a minute, Isabella! I just need to run to the river and fill the gourd." Porkita looked at the hot gourd lying on the ground and tried to figure out how to get it to the river without burning herself. She nudged the gourd with her foot. It moved forward and the quick contact didn't burn her. She gave it a small kick and it flew several feet toward the river. She continued to kick it until she was about ten feet from the river's edge. She tried to give it one last gentle kick, hoping it would land close enough for her to be able to dip it quickly into the river and cool it off, but she kicked too hard and it flew into the swiftly moving water and was swept away.

"Oh, bother! Now what am I going to do?" she asked herself. "Isabella is going to be so mad at me! I've gone and lost our last gourd.

What can I use to gather water for Isabella now?"

As she made her way back to the campsite, Porkita heard Isabella calling.

"Porkita? Are you all right?"

"Yes, Isabella, I am fine."

"What was that strange noise?"

"What noise?" asked Porkita as she searched for something that would hold water.

"It was a thumping noise."

"Oh. That was just me going for water for you."

"May I have some now? My mouth is so dry."

"Um . . . just one minute. It isn't quite ready yet." Wildly searching the area, Porkita grabbed a large, thick leaf and ran to the river's edge. She filled it with the small amount of water that it could hold and hurried back to Isabella. Most of the water dribbled out on the way and there was only a scant mouthful left to give to Isabella.

"May I have some more, please?"

So Porkita ran back and filled it again, succeeding in bringing only a mouthful once more.

"Thank you, Porkita," Isabella said, her voice a little less croaky. "Why don't you just fill the gourd?"

Porkita hung her head in shame. "Oh, Isabella. I'm sorry. I lost the second gourd, too. You see, it was hot from the fire and I couldn't pick it up, so I tried to kick it to the river, and that was the thumping sounds you heard. When I was close to the river, I gave it one last kick and it flew into the water and was lost! I guess I messed up again." Porkita waited for the scolding she felt she deserved.

But instead, Isabella asked, "What fire?" At Porkita's blank stare, she asked again, "You said the gourd was hot from the fire. What fire?"

"The one I built last night to heat water so I could wash your wounds. I also used it to cook some apple stew for you to eat."

Isabella reached for her friend's hand. "You built a fire, cleaned my wounds, and made something hot for us to eat?"

Porkita nodded. "Well, your wounds looked so red and puffy that I thought they should be cleaned. So I built a fire, heated up some water, and used the hot water and soap to clean them. Then I thought you needed to eat something to get your strength back, so I smashed some apples and made apple stew. It didn't look as good as the kind you make, but I fed it to you anyway, a little bit at a time all night long, and now you know who I am again so it must have helped!"

"What do you mean when you say I know who you are again?"

"You didn't know who I was! You tore off your gown and tried to jump in the river! When I stopped you, you fought me. You thought I was the enemy. You said you needed to save some children and . . .

something about your father's soldiers being trees and whiskers and venison. You didn't make any sense! And I was scared to death for you!"

Isabella sighed. "It must have been from the creature's bites. They must have poisoned me. I'm so lucky I had you to take care of me, Porkita! I might have died if you hadn't done all those things for me! Thank you! You saved me from those horrible creatures, and now you've saved me again!"

Porkita's pink skin turned deep red as a blush warmed her face. "Oh, well. I didn't do all that much. I just cleaned your wounds and made you something to eat. But I didn't eat any of the apple stew, even though I was half-starved to death! I saved it all for you!" she announced proudly.

Isabella tried to roll over to embrace her friend, but the effort caused her to moan loudly.

"Isabella! Are you all right? What can I do for you?"

"I'm just very sore and weak, Porkita. I should probably wash my wounds again. Is there anything we can use to heat water?"

"I'll find something, Isabella. Don't worry; I'll take care of it." She rose and started searching the area again. She came back a few minutes later carrying a variety of items.

"Will any of these work?" she asked.

Isabella looked at the collection of leaves, sticks, and rocks. "I'm afraid not, Porkita. You need to find something that is shaped more like the gourd. Something that is bowl-shaped and can hold water. There must be something out there that will work."

Porkita tried again. Several moments later, Isabella heard a joyous, "I found it!" Porkita rushed over to show her a large piece of bark that had fallen off a tree. It was thick and had grown into a shape that would hold water nicely.

"That's perfect, Porkita! Great job! Just be careful not to put it too close to the flames or it might catch on fire."

Porkita spent the rest of the day taking care of Isabella. By the next morning, Isabella could sit up on her own. They rested for another full day, and under Porkita's loving care, Isabella was almost fully recovered by nightfall.

As they sat talking under the stars, Isabella said, "I feel so much better now, Porkita. Thank you for everything."

"I'm glad, Isabella. You look so much better and your wounds are definitely healing. They are only pink now, instead of that reddish purple they were before."

"I think I will always have scars from the wounds, but I think I will be strong enough in the morning to continue our journey. We will need to find some food and then we can follow the river. Hopefully, before long, it will lead us to the mouth of the cave that is the doorway to the Garden of Robyia."

The next morning, the girls packed up their few belongings and walked to the edge of the river.

"Will the river lead us right to the entrance of the Lanolions' land?" asked Porkita.

"Well, no. The river will lead us to the stream that leads to the Lanolions."

"What exactly is a stream?"

"A stream is a smaller vein of water that branches off from the river."

"What if there is more than one stream branching off from this river? How will we know which one is the right one?"

Isabella sighed. "We will have to follow every one of them until we find the right one. But there can't be that many!"

Now it was Porkita's turn to sigh. "Do we even know which way to go here? Do we follow the river this way," she asked, "or that way?"

"This way," answered Isabella, pointing to the right. "Do you see that big hill in the distance? I think that is the Lanolions' home. But the stream is on the other side of the river. We have to get across somehow."

"Just how are we going to do that?" asked Porkita. "It is moving way to fast to walk across, and you know I can't swim!"

"Well, we definitely aren't going to try to cross on any rocks! Do you remember me telling you about my first journey when I tried to walk on the rocks and one turned out to be an animal that rose out of the water to bite me?" Porkita nodded and shivered, glancing at the river to check for any moving rocks. Isabella continued, "But I was able to swing to the other side on a vine. Do you want to try that?"

"What if I fall off or the vine breaks? I'll end up washed away! Isn't there any other way?" begged Porkita.

"Not that I can think of. Can you think of any?"

Porkita sighed and shook her head. "Let's go find a vine, but it had better be a really thick, strong one! And you're going first!"

Once they found vines they felt would work and a jumping off spot, Isabella ran toward the river, and despite her weakened state, swung easily to the other side. Porkita clenched her teeth, and gripping the vine with all her might, ran toward the river. Howling at the top of her lungs, she swung across the river. But she forgot to let go, so she swung right back to where she had begun, her hooves trailing across the top of the water on each pass.

Isabella tried not to laugh at the astonished look on Porkita's face and called, "Try again, Porkita, only this time let go when you reach this side!"

Porkita's second try was successful although she almost landed on top of Isabella. The princesses followed the river, passing several small streams before Isabella cried, "I think this is it, Porkita! I think this one leads to the Lanolions!"

"How can you tell?" Porkita asked. "They all look the same to me."

"Well, I don't know for sure, but it looks familiar and it's heading in the right direction. Let's try it and see."

The bushes and brambles were thick along the edge of the stream and the princesses were soon scratched and frustrated.

"Why don't we take our shoes off and walk in the stream? It's not that deep and all that cold water on my aching feet would feel lovely!" Porkita suggested.

Isabella agreed, so they pulled off their shoes and threw them into the pack. They were able to travel much faster this way, even though the rocks on the bottom of the stream were slippery.

It was late afternoon, and as they came around a bend in the stream, they passed into shadow. Isabella looked up to see what was blocking the sunlight and gasped.

"Porkita! That's it! Up ahead! That's the hill the Lanolions live in! I just know it! Let's hurry."

"I want to hurry, Isabella, really I do. But something's wrong with my feet! I can't seem to feel them. Is that bad?"

"Don't worry, Porkita. It is just from the cold water. Why don't we try to go the rest of the way on land so they will warm up?"

"That sounds good. And as long as we are stopping to dry our feet, let's have a snack. Cold water makes me hungry."

"Here's an apple. Why don't you eat it while we walk? I'm anxious to get there now that we are so close."

The sound of Porkita crunching into the apple mixed with the calls of the birds overhead and the rustle of the leaves as the girls pushed through them. They broke through a last tangle of bushes and reached the foot of the hill. Isabella pulled at the brush until she uncovered the opening to the cave.

"This has to be it! How many other streams lead to a cave in the side of a hill?" asked Isabella.

"Then let's go!" cried Porkita, grabbing Isabella's arm and pulling her toward the opening.

Isabella hesitated. "Um, Porkita, if I knew that something bad may or may not happen, and you didn't know about it, would you want me to tell you or keep it to myself?"

Porkita froze. "What are you talking about?"

"It's just that, after what happened to me last time I came through here, there is a strong possibility that something might be living inside this cave."

Porkita backed up a few steps. "What's living in the cave, Isabella? Tell me."

"I don't know for sure that they are still there"

"They? More than one?" She glanced at the cave and then backed up several more steps.

"Last time there must have been dozens. Maybe hundreds, although it's hard to tell when they are all flying at you at once."

"*Flying at you! Hundreds!* What were they, Isabella?"

"I don't know what they are called. It was dark and I was running and screaming, so I didn't get a really good look at them, but I know they had claws and teeth. They looked kind of like those things that attacked me in the tunnel, only they could fly."

"*And you want me to go in there*? Are you kidding? I'm not going in there!"

"We have to, Porkita. It's the only way to get in to see the Lanolions unless you want to hike all over the top of the hill hoping we get lucky enough to find a hole to fall through," explained Isabella. "Anyway, they didn't hurt me last time. They just flew at me."

"I can't, Isabella. I have tried to be brave and strong like you, I really have, but this is just too much."

"Porkita, you have been very brave and strong! I'm so proud of you! After crawling into that hole and saving me from those creatures, this will be easy! I promise. How about if you pull your skirt over your head and I'll take your hand and lead you through? That way you won't have to see them, and they won't hurt you in any way."

"But what about you? If you don't cover your face, they might attack you!"

"I'll protect my face with my other arm. I'll be fine and so will you. Are you ready?"

Porkita shuddered and flipped her skirt up over her face. She held her hand out and Isabella took it.

Isabella led the way into the dark cave. She hadn't wanted to tell Porkita that she had to run her hand along the slimy cave wall to find her way through the darkness and wouldn't be able to shield her face.

The girls hadn't gone more than two feet into the cave when they heard rustling above their heads.

"Isabella!" Porkita cried out.

The cry was enough to rouse the winged creatures. They dropped from the ceiling to fly at the princesses. Isabella felt their wings bat her face as she dragged Porkita forward. One dug its claws into her scalp and pulled. Isabella knocked it away and kept moving. She could hear Porkita sobbing behind her. The air was full of wings, claws, and screeching.

Isabella stumbled and lost her grip on Porkita. Porkita's screams echoed off the cave walls. Isabella felt around in the darkness for her friend's hand, but the rush of wings at her face kept pushing her backward.

"Porkita! Reach out and try to find my hand!"

Isabella wasn't sure Porkita could even hear her, but a moment later she felt something brush the back of her hand and she latched on to her friend's arm. She stumbled to her feet and hauled Porkita to the faint light at the cave's end. Isabella broke through the branches covering the exit and with one last heave, pulled Porkita to safety.

The winged creatures did not follow them into the light. The girls dropped to the ground, breathing hard and shaking.

As her eyes grew accustomed to the weak light, Isabella had her answer. This was the Garden of Robyia, Home of the Lanolions.

They had made it.

Chapter Fifteen

The Garden of Robyia

"This is it?" Porkita asked when she had caught her breath. "Are you sure?"

"I'm sure," said Isabella. "Can you see that smoke rising up toward the holes where the light is shining in? That is probably the central fire in Inius's village. We should go toward the smoke."

The girls pushed through the bushes, with occasional stops so Porkita could grab berries, and finally reached the circle of huts that were home to the Lanolions. As they entered the clearing, Isabella warned Porkita.

"They might be startled by us. They might scream. Remember, they aren't used to the way we look, and they aren't used to visitors. But don't panic; the Lanolions are very friendly once they get used to you."

Approaching the fire, Isabella heard a small voice call out, "Bella!" One of the youngest Lanolions ran to greet her. Soon the women and children she had befriended on her last journey surrounded her, offering greetings and hugs to Isabella and directing shy glances at Porkita.

Once things settled down, Isabella introduced her. "This is my friend, Princess Porkita of Sowden. She would like to be your friend, too." Porkita was welcomed and both princesses were invited to join the tribe at the central fire.

Isabella asked, "Does anyone know where Inius is? I would like to see him."

A young male Lanolion went to fetch Inius as several of the females brought food to Isabella and Porkita. Porkita dug into the hot meal, but Isabella only took a few nervous bites.

As soon as she caught sight of Inius, Isabella set her plate down and rose to meet him. Porkita stayed seated and rushed to finish her meal.

"Is-a-bella! What are you doing here? I didn't expect to ever see you again," Inius cried as he gave the princess a warm hug.

"I'm so happy to see you again, Inius!" Isabella said in response. "I didn't expect to see you again either, but I had to return. I must talk to Trofmin right away."

Inius's huge round eyes opened even wider, and his horns twitched. "I don't think that is a good idea, Is-a-bella. He wasn't very happy about you coming here last time and he only let you go because you promised never to return. If Trofmin finds out you have come back, he will be very angry."

"I know, Inius, and I meant to keep my promise, but the Lanolions are in danger. I had to come and warn all of you."

"How could the Lanolions be in danger, Is-a-bella? We are safe here in our home within the mountain."

"I really need to see Trofmin. I will explain it to both of you at the same time. Will you take me to him?"

"Will you not listen to reason and leave here before he realizes you have come?"

Isabella shook her head.

Inius sighed. "Then I have no choice but to take you to him. I hope you know what you are doing. He will not be pleased that you have broken your promise. Follow me, my friend Is-a-bella."

Isabella called over her shoulder, "Come on, Porkita. We're going to see the chief."

Inius halted and raised his spear. "Who is this?" he demanded.

Isabella placed her hand on the shaft of the spear. "This is my friend, Princess Porkita of Sowden. She is not a threat. She has traveled very far by my side to help warn you of the danger."

Inius lowered his spear. "Oh, Is-a-bella! Not only have you returned, but you have shown another where we hide. Trofmin will be very angry. You will not like Trofmin when he is angry!" He turned and led the way, shaking his head and muttering as he walked.

Porkita whispered to Isabella, "I thought you said they were friendly! Why is this Trofmin going to be angry? Why didn't they want you to come back? Why did your friend point that spear at me?"

"Not now, Porkita. Everything is going to be fine. Don't worry. We will tell Trofmin what we came to tell him and then we will leave here and find our way home."

Porkita muttered something under her breath.

"What did you say, Porkita?"

"I said, I hope you are right. Somehow it is never as easy as you tell me it is going to be."

As they approached the largest of the many huts, the flap covering its doorway flew up and out strode Trofmin and several other male Lano-lions. The chief had the same narrow chest and wide hips as the rest of the Lanolions, but he was a full head taller than the others. Around his neck hung the star-shaped purple necklace Rankton was so desperate to possess.

Isabella bowed. "Your Highness."

Trofmin stared at her for a moment before replying in his gravelly voice. "You have broken your vow to me, Princess Isabella. You were never to return to the Garden of Robyia."

"I know, Your Highness, but I had a good reason to break my promise to you. The Lanolions are in danger, and I came to give you warning."

The chief's yellow eyes narrowed. "In what way are the Lanolions in danger?"

"This is my friend Princess Porkita of Sowden. I was visiting her kingdom when her whole family was taken captive. A beast called Rankton and his followers had come to Sowden to try to find me. Porkita and I escaped, but Rankton tracked us down. He told us that he wanted me to lead him here, to the home of the Lanolions, so he could take your necklace from you. He said the necklace would give him power over all creatures. We escaped from him once more and then made our way here to warn you."

Trofmin walked in slow circles around Isabella. "How did this Rankton know about the necklace, and why would he think you knew where to find it?" he growled.

"He had heard about the necklace and its power from his father. His

220

father told him the necklace belonged to a tribe who had chosen to make their home underground. When I finally found my home after my last visit here, I told my parents about my travels, including falling through a mountain and finding all of you. One of my father's advisers passed this information on to Rankton."

"And now you have led this Rankton to us."

Isabella protested, "No, Trofmin—"

"Very good, Trofmin. You are smarter than I expected." Stepping out from behind the large hut, Rankton strode to Isabella's side. His followers quickly appeared from behind huts and trees and surrounded the Lanolions, weapons drawn.

"Rankton! H-how did you — w-w-where did you —" Isabella stammered.

"Oh Princess, you are so naive. Did you really think I would just let you go with so much at stake? Did you think you could outsmart Rankton the Ruthless? We saw the smoke from your fire by the river, and we have been following you ever since. I knew sooner or later you would lead us here."

Isabella turned and addressed Trofmin with tears in her eyes. "I am so sorry. I had no idea they were following us. I thought we had gotten rid of them." Trofmin didn't speak or move.

"Enough of the tears and apologies!" roared Rankton. "Trofmin, I have waited a very long time and traveled great distances, and now I will have what should be rightfully mine. Give me the medallion!"

Trofmin's voice was strong as he answered, "You will have to take it from my neck."

Rankton nodded at two of his soldiers who moved to Trofmin's side, their sharp spears aimed at his chest. Rankton stepped forward and lifted the purple medallion over Trofmin's head. Trofmin didn't move a muscle.

Rankton took two steps back then thrust the fist clutching the medallion into the air for all to see. "It is mine. Now all shall bow down before Rankton the Ruthless!" he bellowed. His soldiers cheered and stomped their feet and pushed the Lanolions to their knees.

Isabella waited for Trofmin to fight back. She readied herself to join in if the Lanolions tried to overpower Rankton's men. But no one moved to stop him. Desperate, she threw herself at Rankton and tried to grab the arm holding the necklace, but he used his other arm to swat her away. She jumped up to try again, but two of Rankton's soldiers restrained her.

"Prepare to begin the rule of Rankton the Ruthless!" Rankton yelled as he held the necklace in both hands right above his head. Isabella stared at Trofmin, willing him to do something, anything, but he stood stock still, his face frozen in a mask of indifference.

With a look of complete smugness, Rankton slowly lowered the medallion until it hung down his chest, the purple stone glittering and glowing even more brightly now.

"It is done!" Rankton shouted. "I now have complete domination over all the creatures of the land!"

But something was happening. Isabella noticed the necklace begin to twist and dance around Rankton's neck as he continued his speech. The circle of gold surrounding Rankton's neck was growing smaller and smaller as the chain twisted onto itself.

"All beings will call me king and do my bidding, and you my faithful soldiers will share in the rewards. Not equally, of course, but you shall profit from your ugh — eeeeh —"

The necklace was now wrapped so tight, it was choking Rankton. He tore at it, gasping, but it only seemed to grow tighter. He flailed about trying to dislodge it, his eyes bulging, his face blue.

The guards restraining Isabella dropped her arms and stepped back in horror. But none of Rankton's soldiers stepped forward to help him. Some of them turned and ran.

Isabella rushed to his side and tried to loosen the chain, but it was so tight she couldn't force her fingers between the chain and Rankton's neck. Rankton pushed her aside and clawed at his neck with his remaining strength. The chain didn't budge.

Rankton's body hit the ground so hard that the pots by the fire rattled. The necklace flew off and landed in the dirt next to him. Isabella ran forward and knelt by his side. She tipped his head back and saw his unblinking eyes. She pounded on his back with both her fists.

"You can't help him, Princess. He is dead." Trofmin told her, calmly. These words sent the rest of Rankton's soldiers scurrying off into the forest.

Isabella looked up at Trofmin, horrified. "You killed him!"

"I didn't kill him, Isabella. The evil in his heart killed him."

"What did you do to the necklace to make it act like that?"

"*I* didn't do anything."

"Then why did it choke him?"

"This necklace was created a very long time ago. It was made by one of the most powerful sorcerers ever born. His name was Nalascar, and he made it for the ruler of that time, King Tiben. King Tiben was a very good king who took care of his subjects and ruled fairly and well. There had been many rulers before Tiben who had treated their subjects cruelly, and Nalascar was sure there would more wicked rulers after Tiben."

Trofmin bent and picked up the necklace. "Nalascar decided to create this medallion to ensure that King Tiben and his heirs would always rule over the land. Rankton was right when he said that the medallion gave power over all beings. If I was wearing the necklace and told you to bow before me, you would. If I told you to hand over all that you own, you would. You simply wouldn't be able to stop yourself from obeying my every command."

Isabella winced. "Imagine Rankton with that kind of power! No wonder he wanted it so badly!"

Trofmin nodded. "But Rankton's father must not have told him everything. He must not have told him about the curse. You see, although King Tiben was a good man, even good men can be tempted. So after Nalascar gave him the medallion, he started to have brief moments of wondering what it would be like if he used the medallion's power to own everything, to make others obey his every command. Soon these fleeting thoughts were coming more and more often, keeping him awake at night, scaring him. So he asked Nalascar to put a curse on the necklace."

"What kind of curse?" asked Isabella.

"If a truly just creature with a pure heart wears the medallion, a creature who cares more for others than for himself, no harm will come to him. But if it is worn by one whose heart is full of greed, who only seeks to use the necklace to hurt and control others for his own profit, then the necklace will kill him."

"If the necklace was made for King Tiben and his heirs, why do you have it?"

"Because King Tiben feared the necklace and the thoughts it put into his head. He asked a trusted friend to take the necklace to a place where it would never be found. That friend was Oklis, the father of my father's father. Oklis gathered the guards he trusted most and along with their families, they traveled here to patiently hollow out this mountain and make a safe home for themselves. It is safe for us to wear the medallion because we have no wish to rule over anyone. Our only desire is to live here in peace."

"King Tiben must have trusted Oklis very much to give him the necklace."

"The legend passed down through my family is that Oklis was not King Tiben's first choice. He placed the necklace around the necks of two others before Oklis."

"What happened to them?" asked Porkita, her ears twitching in curiosity.

"They died in much the same way Rankton did. Perhaps not as quickly since their greed wasn't as great as his."

Isabella stood. "That necklace should never have been created! Even if you are good and true, you shouldn't have that kind of power! And even if you are as evil as Rankton, you shouldn't have to die like that! No good can come from that necklace!"

226

Trofmin nodded. "Maybe you are right. Maybe Nalascar made a mistake when he conjured up this necklace, but what's done is done. And our only choice now is to continue to protect the necklace at all costs."

Porkita stepped forward. "Excuse me, but if the necklace would kill any evil being that would steal it and put it on, why is it so important to protect it?"

"Because," explained Trofmin, "no spell is foolproof. Someday, someone will find a way around the curse. And that kind of power in the wrong hands would be a disaster."

"Why don't we just destroy it?" asked Porkita.

"The necklace is indestructible."

"We could throw it in a lake or bury it somewhere," Porkita suggested.

"Then there would always be the possibility it could be found. We can't take that chance. Better to know that it is safe than wonder always if it has been found. Princess Isabella, you are awfully quiet. What are you thinking?"

Isabella looked him square in the eye. "I'm wondering why you didn't use the necklace's power to stop Rankton. You could have ordered him and his soldiers to leave, and he wouldn't have had to die. Why didn't you?"

Trofmin returned her stare. "I have never used the necklace to control others. I never will. Neither did my father, or his father, or his father before him. It is not mine to use, it is simply mine to protect. Just as someday my son and his son after him will guard this necklace. It is our destiny."

"But you rule over the Lanolions here in the garden. Don't they have to obey your orders because you wear the necklace?" Isabella asked.

"I do not rule over the Lanolions. All here have a say in decisions affecting the tribe. We meet regularly at the central fire and make decisions as a group. Just as we will have to meet to decide how we are going to protect the necklace now that outsiders know about it and its hiding place. Inius, will you please gather the tribe so we can discuss what has happened?"

Inius bowed and left.

Isabella watched Inius leave and then turned back to Trofmin. "I guess Porkita and I will leave you to your decisions. We have a long journey back to our homes to make sure our families are safe."

Trofmin clamped a hand onto her shoulder. "Not quite yet, Princess. You have brought trouble into our land even though you promised never to return. The tribe will have to decide what is to be done with you." He guided her firmly to the central fire where the rest of the Lanolions were gathering.

Porkita slipped in beside Isabella and took her hand. "Whatever they decide, we're in this together," she whispered. Isabella squeezed her hand.

Once the tribe had settled, Trofmin pulled a brightly colored pole out of the ground and spoke. "Lanolions, we have a difficult situation to resolve. Princess Isabella of Grom, who accidentally stumbled across our land once before, has returned, this time bringing with her outsiders who tried to take the Medallion of Tiben. Princess Isabella says she came to warn us about these thieves and did not know that they had followed her here. But the thieves only knew about our existence because the princess told others about our secret land. We must decide how we will protect the medallion now that so many know it exists and where to find it, and we must decide what punishment, if any, the Princess is to receive for revealing our secrets and bringing danger to our land."

Trofmin held the pole out to Isabella. "You may tell your story first, Princess. Only the one holding the pole may speak."

Isabella took the pole and faced the Lanolions. The faces that had looked so welcoming earlier now looked troubled. "First I would like to apologize for the trouble I have caused all of you. I never meant to put you in danger. I fell into your land by accident last time, and you were so nice to me. I planned to honor Trofmin's wishes and never return. I didn't think I could find my way back even if I wanted to. But then everything changed."

"When I got back home, I told everyone about my adventures. I told them about you because I wanted them to know that even though we are different, we could still be friends. And since no one knew where your mountain was, I thought it was safe to talk about you. But someone told Rankton what I said. He arranged for me to travel alone to Porkita's kingdom for a wedding. Then he captured Porkita's family and tied them to chairs." There were gasps from some of the female Lanolions.

"He was trying to kidnap me to make me tell him where you lived, but Porkita and I escaped. He tracked us down and threatened our families if we didn't show him how to get here. So we took him as far away from here as we could until we were able to escape again. Then we hurried here to warn you."

Tears filled Isabella's eyes. "It was my idea to come here. I thought we could sneak here without his knowing about it and tell you that he was looking for you. I guess it was a bad idea. I swear to you that I didn't know he had followed us, or I would have led him away from here again. I would never willingly put any of you in danger. And if I'm allowed to go home, I will never try to return here again. I'm sorry." Isabella couldn't look into their faces any longer, so she dropped her gaze to her feet.

Porkita reached out to touch the pole and say, "It's my fault, too. If I hadn't lit a fire by the river, Rankton wouldn't have found us and followed us."

Almost immediately the pole was taken from her hands and Inius came to Isabella's defense. "I-sa-bella wasn't trying to help the thieves. She was trying to help us. It isn't her fault they were tricky enough to follow her. I say we let her and her friend go free."

A female Lanolion grabbed the pole. "I agree. Isabella isn't a thief. She didn't try to take the necklace. The one who did is dead and can't harm us anymore."

A large male pushed his way forward to take the pole and say, "She's not a thief, but she did lead the thieves here. If we let her go, she might do it again."

The tiny female Lanolion that had called to Isabella when she arrived reached for the pole simply to say, "Bella is my friend." Then she dropped the pole to the ground and ran to hug Isabella's leg.

A few more Lanolions stepped forward to voice their opinions, most of them forgiving of Isabella.

When no one else stepped up to speak, Trofmin took the speaking stick. "I have listened to all of you, and I agree with those who say she is not a thief. But we have problems to resolve. Rankton is dead, that is true. But all his soldiers know the legend of the necklace, and they know where our home is. How long do you think it will be before one of them decides to come back for it? And some of you obviously don't trust Princess Isabella when she says she will never come here again. Therefore, we need to come up with a solution that keeps the necklace and all of us safe. Does anyone have any ideas about that?"

The Lanolions murmured among themselves, but no one came forward to take the pole.

"I have an idea," said Trofmin, "but it will have to be agreed on by the whole tribe. I believe that we are no longer safe here in our garden. I think as long as we remain here, there will always be outsiders coming here to try and steal the necklace. I think the tribe must move to a new home."

After the exclamations of shock, Isabella heard, "But this has always been our home!" and "Where would we go?" along with "Is there no other way?"

Trofmin raised his hand for silence. "I don't see any other way. As our ancestors did before us, we will have to find a new home that is a safe hiding place for the necklace, a home that no outsiders know about, including Princess Isabella. Wiggle your horns if you agree." Isabella saw all the horns wiggle, although some less enthusiastically than others.

"Then it is agreed," stated Trofmin. "I have one more suggestion. But since there may be thieves still lingering in our garden, I hesitate to speak it out loud. I shall write it on the ground and each of you will come forward to read it. If you agree, make a mark in the dirt beside it."

Trofmin wrote for awhile in the dirt and then the Lanolions came one at a time to read his suggestion. Isabella watched as one after another made a mark of agreement. Inius was the last Lanolion to vote, and he stared sadly at Isabella for a moment before making a slight mark in the dirt.

Porkita was fidgeting with curiosity beside her, but Isabella was feeling too guilty at her part in forcing the Lanolions to leave their home to care what was written in the dirt. So she was startled when Trofmin called her forward to read his words, and even more startled to see her name written there.

"Since Princess Isabella had a major role in putting the Medallion of Tiben at risk and since there are bound to be thieves lurking nearby still plotting to steal the necklace from the Lanolions, I propose that I take Princess Isabella into my hut and place the necklace around her neck. If she proves trustworthy and lives, she will sneak the necklace back to her kingdom and keep it safely there until we are settled in our new home. At that time a Lanolion will visit her and retrieve the necklace and bring it safely back where it belongs."

"No! I don't want to!"

"Silence! Don't say another word out loud. Marmin, wipe out those words in the dirt, please, then set up a guard to protect the village. Isabella, we will continue this conversation in private. Follow me."

Isabella followed Trofmin and two of his guards into his hut. Out of the corner of her eye, she saw Inius slip in behind them.

"Now, Princess, what were you about to say?"

"I don't want to take the necklace! I don't want anything to do with it!"

"You have to take it. You owe it to us," insisted Trofmin.

"But what if I lose it? What if Rankton's soldiers follow me and try to take it? Why do you think it will be safer with me than with you?"

"They won't expect us to give it to you. They think we are mad at you and don't trust you. We will fake a scene by the fire to further this belief. Then we will send you away in disgrace with the necklace safely hidden beneath your gown. After a day or two, we will leave. Hopefully, those who still seek the necklace will wait to follow us and won't be interested in your departure. We will have a long journey trying to lose those who follow us and find a new home. I am convinced the medallion will be safer with you. You must travel straight to your home and the protection of your father's soldiers."

"I don't think it will be safer with me! Do you know what I have gone through on my journeys? You have been shut up inside this mountain since you were born. Do you have any idea what is waiting on the outside? There are giant hairy beasts, biting rocks, spitting frogs, and all kinds of dangers out there! What if I am killed? Then what happens to the necklace? At least if the necklace is with all of you and you are killed, another Lanolion can take it to its new home. It makes more sense for you to take it."

Trofmin grabbed her shoulders. "It is not for you to decide. The Lanolions have voted and decided you are to take the necklace for now. If you wish to leave our land, it will be with the necklace around your neck. It is your way to repair all the damage you have done."

Isabella's shoulders drooped and Trofmin added, "That is, if it doesn't kill you first."

Chapter Sixteen

Heading for Home

"Are you ready, Princess?"

Isabella nodded.

Trofmin held out the necklace and Isabella took it. It was heavier than she expected and felt warm in her hands.

"What do I do now?" she asked.

"Simply place it around your neck. If you are truly only concerned with helping others, you will be fine. But if you have greed and a desire to use the necklace for your own power, it will dance and shimmer and eventually choke you to death."

Porkita moved closer to Isabella and said, "I know what's in your heart, Isabella. You have nothing to fear. Put it on."

Isabella gave Porkita a small smile and lowered the necklace around her neck. It didn't dance. It didn't shimmer. It just lay on her chest looking as ordinary as the necklaces her mother wore everyday.

"Very good, Princess. It pleases me to know you were telling the truth about not leading the thieves to our land. And now I am even more certain you are the right person to keep the necklace safe for us until we are ready for it."

Isabella answered, "I do not agree, but I will do as you ask."

"Now," said Trofmin, "if you would slip the necklace under your gown so it can't be seen, we will join the others by the fire and I will pretend to banish you from us forever. Then you and Princess Porkita should leave and hurry home to your kingdom and the safety of your father's guards. One more thing, Princess, do not tell anyone of the necklace's power. Not even your parents. It is to remain around your neck until a Lanolion comes to reclaim it. Do you understand?"

Isabella replied, "I understand and give you my word."

Trofmin turned to Porkita. "Do you also give your word that you will not tell anyone about the necklace's power?"

Porkita swallowed hard and nodded.

237

Trofmin nodded once and said, "Then this is goodbye. We will act out our scene for the enemy, and I will never see the two of you again. Take care of yourselves. I wish you both long and happy lives."

"We wish the same for you, Trofmin," said Isabella, "and for all your tribe."

Inius stepped forward from the shadows and hugged Isabella. "Goodbye, Is-a-bella, and take care of yourself. I will always remember you and will tell my sons and daughters about you."

"Goodbye, Inius. You are a good and true friend, and I will always remember you, too."

The girls followed Trofmin from the hut, the necklace safely hidden beneath Isabella's gown. Trofmin called to the tribe to gather around the fire.

Trofmin yelled his speech so that all who might be listening would hear. "Friends, Princess Isabella of Grom has shamed herself and her tribe by breaking her promise never to return to the Garden of Robyia and by leading a band of thieves into our midst. She has brought danger upon us and betrayed us with her actions. Therefore, she is to be banished from our sight, and if she should ever try to return to the land of the Lanolions, she will be immediately killed. Leave us now, Princess Isabella, for in our hearts and eyes, you no longer exist." Trofmin turned his back on her and one by one the other Lanolions did the same. Soon, there were only two still facing the girls — Inius and the little female who had made friends with Isabella. With a last look, Inius picked the little one up and turned away.

Isabella and Porkita crept through the bushes, watching for any of Rankton's soldiers. When they found the entrance to the cave, Porkita silently took Isabella's hand and steeled herself to enter. But when they did, there was no rush of wings and claws. Instead there were hundreds of the creatures dead or injured on the ground.

Porkita screamed and Isabella hugged her tight. "It must have been Rankton and his soldiers. Let's just try to hurry through."

As they exited the cave, Porkita asked, "Do you even know how to get to our kingdoms from here?"

"I think I can find my way. Should we go to your kingdom or mine?"

"I want to go to mine and make sure my family is safe," answered Porkita. "I can't take not knowing anymore. Lyalus was going to your kingdom to tell them about the poison, so your family's most likely safe, but for all I know, my family might still be tied to chairs or worse!"

"I agree. As much as I want to see my parents, I think it is more important to make sure your family is all right. Also, Grammy's is on the way to your castle, so we can stop and make sure Rankton's goons didn't hurt her."

"Then let's go! Which way?" Porkita asked.

"We have to follow the stream to the river, then follow the river to the valley that leads to the Gorilmen's tall trees, then there is the swamp, the bushes that rustle, and that takes us to Grammy's. After Grammy's, we have to go over that big mountain where we met that crazy two-faced bird; then we will be at your door."

"It's getting pretty dark," Porkita said. "Do you think we should stop for the night?"

"Let's just follow the stream back to the river and set up camp there." They made their way back to the river without any problems and settled in for the night.

After a quick breakfast, the girls followed the river, being very careful to avoid any holes that might lead to the furry creatures' tunnels. They found the spot where they crossed the river last time and used vines to cross again.

"Isabella, as much as I enjoyed visiting the Gorilmen last time, I want to go home. I don't feel like wasting time coming up with some act to entertain them. Can't we go around the tall trees?"

Isabella pointed at the forest. "Look how big their forest is. It would take us forever to go around it. I don't feel like being held captive by them either, but it would probably be quicker than trying to find a way around their home. Maybe we'll have better luck sneaking through this time. Let's go through the bushes instead of down the path."

The girls started to push through the bushes as quietly as they could, but only made it halfway through the tall trees before they heard something coming behind them.

"Run, Porkita!" Isabella screamed. "Don't look back, just run!"

The princesses veered onto the path and took off running, screaming at the top of their lungs. Isabella weaved from one side of the path to the other to make it harder for the Gorilmen to grab her. She could hear Porkita's hooves pounding the dirt right behind her.

She stopped screaming to take a breath and heard a voice call, "Princess Isabella! Stop! Princess Porkita!" Isabella chanced a quick look over her shoulder, then stopped so quickly Porkita slammed into her and knocked her to the ground.

Untangling herself from Porkita, Isabella looked to make sure she had really seen what she'd thought she'd seen.

"Mystic! It's really you!" Isabella jumped up and threw her arms around Mystic's neck. "Where did you come from? How are our families? Have you seen my parents?"

Porkita still sat on the hard ground, just staring at the magical creature that had protected her family for so many years.

"I will answer all your questions, I promise. But now we have to get out of here before the Gorilmen detain us. Quick, jump on my back, both of you!"

Mystic knelt and Isabella slipped on to her back. She held her hand out to Porkita, who finally gained her senses and scrambled on behind her. Mystic stood and then moved rapidly down the path, her hooves barely brushing the ground.

"They're coming after us!" Porkita warned.

Isabella looked back to see five or six Gorilmen swinging from vine to vine, getting closer with every swing.

"Hurry, Mystic! They're catching up!" she yelled.

Looking ahead, Isabella saw faint beams of light filtering through the trees and knew that they were almost to the end of the Gorilmen's territory. But she also saw four Gorilmen swinging toward them. She heard bursts of laughter echoing through the trees.

Mystic dodged around the swinging monkey men and with her head down, burst through the opening into the meadow. Once she was beyond the reach of the Gorilmen, she slowed and stopped, allowing the princesses to slide from her back.

Isabella looked back at the forest to see Argulan and a few members of his tribe standing in the shadows.

"I'm sorry, Argulan. We don't mean to offend you, but we don't have time to entertain you today. We need to return to our kingdoms and make sure our families are safe," Isabella called.

Argulan smiled. "No offense taken, Princess. And you are wrong. You did have time. Trying to catch you and your friends was very entertaining! May your journey be safe." With that, he and his tribesmen disappeared into the trees.

Isabella gave Mystic a moment to catch her breath, then peppered her with questions. "What's going on? Were you able to free Porkita's family? Did Lyalus reach my kingdom and warn my father? Is everyone safe?"

"Why don't we sit for a moment? Knowing her as I do, I'm sure Princess Porkita would like something to eat while I tell you what has been happening," Mystic suggested.

Dropping to the ground, Porkita complained, "Who cares about food? Tell us about our families, please."

Isabella quickly sat beside her and Mystic began. "Your families are all safe. They are all waiting for you to return. There are soldiers from both kingdoms searching frantically for the two of you."

Isabella wrapped a squealing Porkita in a tight hug. "Oh, Mystic!" Isabella cried. "That is the best news! We've been so worried!"

"Not as worried as we have all been about the two of you. Lyalus told us Rankton and his soldiers had captured you. How did you manage to escape?"

"Um," Isabella stalled, casting a glance at Porkita, "we were crossing a rope bridge and it broke, stranding us on one side of a canyon and Rankton and his troops on the other. But I want to hear more about what happened in Sowden. Did my father's guards free the royal family?"

"They didn't have to. When you two escaped, Rankton took most of his soldiers with him. He only left a handful to guard the royals, a few more to guard the gates of the kingdom, and several to guard the staff. I spent the first few days snooping around. I found out that your family, Porkita, was still tied to chairs in the dining room with three guards always watching them. I also found out that most of the servants and your father's guards were locked in the third floor ballroom except for four of the cooks who were brought down to the kitchen to cook meals for Rankton's guards."

"Who cooked for my family and the rest of the staff?" asked Porkita.

"No one. The soldiers just threw a bag of moldy corn on the floor for the staff and guards to eat, and they pushed your family's chairs up to the table and scattered some fruit across it, but they didn't untie their hands so eating was difficult."

"Those animals!" cried Porkita.

"Don't worry, Princess. They got what they deserved."

"What happened?" asked Isabella.

"When one of the cooks came out to the garden to gather supplies, I hid in the thicket and whispered a plan to her. I told her to put something in the guard's meal that evening that would make them ill. I had hidden a bottle of herbs in the pantry that would do the job. She agreed to the plan. That night, one by one, Rankton's guards ended up on the ground, writhing in agony and holding their stomachs. While they were in too much pain to care what I was up to, I snuck up to the ballroom and freed the staff and guards of Sowden. We raced down to the dining room to free your family and found that they had already freed themselves!"

"How?" asked Porkita, finally helping herself to an apple from Grammy's pack.

Mystic chuckled. "Rankton's soldiers made a mistake when they didn't make sure your family was well-fed. Hogitha got so hungry she chewed through your father's ropes! He was then able to untie the rest of the family and when we got there, they were sitting at the table eating all the fruit they couldn't reach when their hands had been tied! Meanwhile, Rankton's thugs were collapsed on the floor. We tied all of them up and stuck them in the dungeon."

"I didn't even know we had a dungeon," exclaimed Porkita. "So my family is really okay?"

"They are fine. Once he wasn't starving anymore, your father immediately organized a search party to come look for you and Isabella. He wanted to lead it himself, but I convinced him to wait at the palace and let me lead the guards. I sent guards in four different directions since I had no idea where you were. I led a group toward your kingdom, Princess Isabella, but I hadn't gone far when I ran into Lyalus. He had brought half your father's army to rescue the Kingdom of Sowden. The other half was out looking for you two."

Isabella smiled. "I knew I could count on Lyalus. So what happened next?"

"We decided to split your father's soldiers up and send them in different directions to look for you, too. We have been looking for weeks without any luck and then today, I had a vision and just like that, I knew where you would be. Now, tell me what happened to the two of you and why Rankton wanted you to begin with."

Porkita and Isabella exchanged nervous glances before Isabella said, "Would you mind if that waited? We are so anxious to go home and I'm sure our families are worried sick. Could we wait and tell everyone about it at the same time?"

Mystic studied the princesses' faces before answering, "Of course, Your Highnesses. Whatever you wish. Let us be on our way, then. If it is all right with you, I will take you back to where I left the search party. That way I can send some of them to Grom to collect Princess Isabella's parents and they can meet us at the Kingdom of Sowden."

"That would be wonderful, Mystic," answered Isabella, "but can we make one stop on our way to Sowden?"

"As you wish, Your Highness."

When they reached the search party, Mystic divided up the guards, sending four to Grom, keeping ten and a coach to escort the princesses home and then dispatching the rest in different directions to gather up the troops who were still searching.

The trip was much faster now that they were riding in the royal coach. They flew past the sinking sand of the swamp and then around the bushes that rustle, and by sunset they were at Grammy's door. Sitting on the porch in her favorite rocker was Grammy.

"Lands sake, child, you've showed up at my door in a lot of different ways, but this is a first! What are ya up ta now?"

Isabella and Porkita ran up the steps to embrace the old woman. Isabella rushed to tell her, "We're going home, Grammy! We're finally going home, and we're taking you with us!"

"What are ya talking about, girl?"

"Rankton is dead and his soldiers are scattered everywhere. This is our friend Mystic. Mystic found us and led us to our fathers' guards, and they are escorting us back to Porkita's kingdom. It's right over this mountain. We want you to come with us. Then I want you to travel with me back to my kingdom and stay with us. Will you?"

Porkita chimed in. "Please, Grammy? We really want you to."

Grammy touched each of them on their cheek. "Ya'll are so sweet. But I can't go to no palace. I don't have nothing to wear, and I wouldn't know how ta act around yer parents and all. I'm better off staying right here with Orion. But you girls are welcome to visit any time ya like."

Porkita offered, "Your clothes are fine, Grammy, and if you want, you may borrow a gown from me or my sisters when we get to the palace. You can borrow as many as you want. I'll have the royal dressmaker sew a dozen just for you. Please come with us!"

Isabella added, "And we don't want you to act like anybody, just be yourself. Our parents will want to meet the women who has helped us so many times."

Grammy hesitated and the girls tugged at her arms and begged, "Ple-e-e-ase!"

Grammy gave in. "I can't resist both of ya when yer begging like a gander on the chopping block."

Porkita looked at Isabella. "Does that mean she's coming or not coming?"

"She's coming!"

The princesses helped Grammy pack up a few possessions and got her settled in the royal coach. They tried to convince Orion to ride on their laps in the coach, but he preferred flying overhead.

The ride over the mountain rattled their bones, but they hardly noticed as they spent the time catching up. The moonlight rippled off Mystic's pearly coat as she kept pace alongside the coach, eyes always alert for any sign of danger.

As they traveled the road that led to the castle gates, a cloud of dust signaled their arrival. By the time they stopped, Porkita's whole family and most of the residents of the castle were waiting to welcome them.

Queen Hogalynn had Porkita in her arms before her hooves hit the ground. "My baby! Are you all right? Let me look at you. What did they do to you? You are positively skin and bones!"

King Hamlet was next to embrace Porkita as the queen fussed over Isabella. Both girls were passed around for hugs from everyone. With everyone talking at once, it was a few minutes before Isabella remembered Grammy.

Isabella found her standing next to the coach, smiling as she watched the happy reunion.

"Everybody! May I have your attention? I would like to introduce a very good friend of Porkita's and mine. She helped us greatly when we were running away from Rankton and his soldiers. King Hamlet and Queen Hogalynn, princesses, members of the royal court, may I present . . ." She whispered to Grammy, "How should I introduce you?"

Grammy whispered back, "Oh, jus' Grammy will do fine."

Isabella smiled. "May I present Grammy!"

Porkita's family stepped forward to warmly welcome Grammy and thank her for all the help she gave the girls.

"Oh my," said Grammy, giggling, "I've never met a real King and Queen before. I'm more nervous than-than-well, I'm too nervous to think what I'm more nervous than!" The royals chuckled with delight.

"Let's move this party inside," suggested the King, his arm around Porkita. "We'll have a feast to celebrate the girls' safe return, Grammy's visit, and the end of this nightmare. Besides, I can't wait to hear what the girls have to tell us!"

Porkita and Isabella exchanged worried glances as the group moved into the castle.

"Father, do you think you and mother could entertain Grammy while Isabella and I take a bath and change?" Porkita asked.

"Of course, of course, my dear. That's a splendid idea. We'll get to know Grammy, you'll get cleaned up, and the servants will prepare the feast. Run along now."

Porkita grabbed Isabella's hand and the two sprinted to the bedroom they would share once again.

"Before the nurses come to help us get cleaned up," Porkita suggested, "we should figure out what we're going to tell everyone. They're going to have a lot of questions."

"I know," responded Isabella. "And we absolutely can't say anything about the necklace. What are we going to tell them?"

"Wait!" cried Porkita. "What did you tell Lyalus when he snuck into camp that night? Did you tell him about the necklace? Because if you did, he might have already told you father."

Isabella thought for a moment. "I can't remember. I know I told him Rankton wanted me to lead him to the Lanolions, but I don't know if I told him about the necklace. It was late, and he was only there for a few minutes. I'm just not sure."

"I don't want to lie to my parents."

"Neither do I. But I can't break my promise to the Lanolions. What a mess!"

Three nurses entered and began to fill the tub.

"Let's think about it while we take our baths. Do you want to go first?" asked Isabella..

"No, you go ahead. I think I'll have a little snack while I wait for my turn."

The nurses wouldn't leave until both girls had been cleaned, powdered, perfumed, and dressed in elaborate gowns.

"Finally!" Porkita exclaimed when the nurses left, "I thought they would never finish. I missed being home, and I missed the royal feasts, but it was kind of nice not to have to have them fussing over me for a few weeks!"

"I know what you mean. Who cares about ringlets in your hair and how many bows are on your gown when there are monsters like Rankton running around?"

"Did you come up with a plan?" asked Porkita.

"Not really. I guess we just have to stick as close to the truth as we can without betraying the Lanolions. We could tell them Rankton wanted us to lead him to the Lanolions because they had something he wanted, but we don't have to tell them what it was. Then we could say that when we found the Lanolions, he collapsed and died and his troops scattered. What do you think?"

Porkita shrugged. "I don't know what else we can do. I guess we'll have to try that. Let's go."

The girls joined the party in the royal dining room. Grammy was entertaining everyone with stories while the servants laid out the feast. Once everyone was seated and had filled their plates, all eyes turned to Isabella and Porkita.

"Well," Isabella began, "we were in the kitchen making a wedding gift for Hogitha and—"

"Really?" squealed Hogitha. "What was it?"

"It was some of those candies you like. So we went up the back stairs to—"

Hogitha stood up. "Are they still down there? In the kitchen?"

"What?"

"The candies you made for me? Are they still in the kitchen?"

King Hamlet took control. "Hogitha, we would like to hear about what happened to Porkita and Isabella. You can check later and see if the candies are there. Please continue, Isabella."

Isabella told them about seeing the family tied to chairs and how they escaped through the back door. She told them about finding Mystic tied up in the shed and the map Mystic drew for them. Occasionally, Porkita interrupted to add a detail or two. Between the two of them, they managed to describe the whole ordeal, talking a lot about the creatures they met and glossing over the reason why Rankton was after Isabella in the first place. Grammy and the royal family groaned and gasped during the story, and once Queen Hogalynn rushed over to hug both of the girls, but they didn't ask questions until the girls were finished.

". . . and then Mystic found us and here we are!" finished Isabella.

King Hamlet filled his plate for the fourth time and said, "But I still don't understand what these Lanolions had that Rankton wanted badly enough to go through all of this! He must have said something about what he was looking for. Didn't he even give you a clue?"

Isabella looked at Porkita. Porkita looked at Isabella. Then she took a deep breath and said, "Father, we do know what Rankton wanted. We know exactly what he wanted. But we made a promise to the Lanolions that we would never tell anyone what it was."

"Besides," added Isabella, "if I hadn't told everyone about the Lano-lions' secret home the first time, Rankton would never have come after me. We can't tell anyone this time."

King Hamlet blurted, "Not even me? But I'm your father, Porkita. And a KING!"

Porkita shook her head. "Not even you, Father. We promised. And a royal princess never goes back on her word." Her eyes asked him to trust her.

The king shook his head and smiled. "I guess our youngest daughter has grown up a bit while she was away. Traipsing all over the land trying to outwit Rankton and his soldiers, being terrorized by spitting frogs and biting rocks, and then saving your best friend's life! Why, I guess if you could do all that, you could do just about anything!" he said proudly.

Porkita turned to Isabella and winked. "I'm glad you think so, Father. I've decided I'd like to study acting."

King Hamlet flinched as though someone had taken a punch at him. "Impossible! No royal ever-in the great history of Sowden-unheard of..."

Queen Hogalynn waved to one of the maids. "Please bring the King a large plate of sweetened pears. In fact, bring the whole pan. He's going to need it." When it arrived he was still blustering, but the queen patted him on the back and spoon-fed him pears until he calmed down.

Later, lying in bed, Isabella murmured sleepily, "Your father was right, Porkita. Just think what your life was like back when you spent all of your days getting beauty treatments! Now you can read, cook meals, start a fire, take care of someone who is injured, and solve difficult problems! Not to mention your amazing acting ability!"

Porkita giggled but it came out as a snort. "And it's all thanks to you, Isabella. If you hadn't shown up at our door, I would still be sitting in a chair all day getting my hair and nails done, with a mud pack on my face! I would have never had the courage to tell my father what I really wanted. Of course, if it weren't for you, I wouldn't have almost died crossing that rope bridge, and been scarred for life by frog spit, and got stuck in a bathtub and—"

Isabella laughed and elbowed her friend in her well padded side. "All right, all right, I get the point! Good night, Porkita."

The next morning, the nurses insisted on fussing over the girls for awhile, trying to repair the damage to their skin, hair, and nails. Porkita's was only temporary and she would soon be back to normal, but Isabella had added a couple of scars, especially where the stones had been embedded in her flesh.

They spent the afternoon chatting with Grammy and answering more questions from the family about their adventure. Every few minutes, Queen Hogalynn had the servants bring a fresh tray of food to tempt Porkita and Isabella. Isabella only picked at the treats, but Porkita was working hard to replace the pounds she had lost on the journey.

There was a great commotion in front of the palace right as the evening feast was about to begin. Isabella ran to the gates, expecting to see her parents, but was not prepared for the visitor who stepped out of the fancy carriage instead.

Isabella let out a heart-stopping scream and fainted dead away.

Chapter Seventeen

Until Death Do Us Part

Isabella woke up to find herself cradled on Grammy's lap with a lot of worried faces staring down at her.

"Land's sakes, child! You gived us quite a scare! Are you all right now?" asked Grammy.

Isabella reached for her friend. "Porkita! Did you see him? He's back! He's come back for us!"

Porkita knelt down and took Isabella's hand. "Who's back, Isabella? What are you talking about?"

Isabella grew even paler as she answered, "Rankton. He's back. I saw him get out of a carriage. Didn't any of you see him?" She scanned the crowd above her for an answer, then screamed once more.

"There he is! He's right there!" she yelled, pointing at a large gray creature with a snout and pointed ears.

Porkita stroked her hair. "No, Isabella. That's not Rankton. That's Hogitha's fiancé, Prince Hogden. Hogden, come closer. Look at his eyes. They aren't small and mean like Rankton's."

Prince Hogden slowly lowered his considerable bulk next to Isabella. She could instantly see that he wasn't anything like Rankton. His eyes were warm and kind and the skin next to them crinkled as he smiled at her.

"I'm sorry to have given you such a fright, Princess Isabella," he said in a voice that reminded Isabella of warm syrup. "And I'm very sorry I didn't realize how evil Rankton was. If I had known, I would have made sure he never saw the outside of my dungeon. I knew he had some crazy ideas, but I never thought he would act on them."

"That's all right," Isabella said, sitting up. "It wasn't your fault. It must have just been a trick of the light. Now that I see you up close, I can see you look nothing like Rankton. How did you know what happened?"

"Mystic dispatched a messenger to my kingdom to tell me what the situation was. I came as quickly as I could."

Hogden rose, with the help of several guards, just in time to have Hogitha launch herself into his arms. "Hogden! Thank goodness you're here! It's been a nightmare! Let's go into dinner and I'll tell you everything that has happened." She took his arm and led him into the palace.

Porkita helped Isabella slowly stand up. "Are you sure you are all right? Do you need anything?"

Isabella shook her head. "The only thing I need now is to see my parents."

Everyone drifted back inside to enjoy the evening's feast.

As the last of the empty platters were cleared away, King Hamlet asked, "So, what are we going to do about this wedding, Hogden?"

Hogden swallowed the last of his food, took Hogitha's hand, and answered, "I was hoping we could be married tomorrow. I know it is too late to invite all the original guests, but I don't want to wait any longer. I want Hogitha to be my bride."

King Hamlet raised his bushy eyebrows at Hogitha, and she nodded vigorously. He then turned to Queen Hogalynn. "What do you think, dear? Can we pull off a wedding fit for a princess by tomorrow?"

She smiled. "We can. It will be a small wedding, but it will be lovely." She turned to the bride-to-be. "Hogitha, you had better fill your plate one more time if you expect to fill out the beautiful gown you chose for your wedding. This ordeal has burned off some of your lovely weight."

"Yes, mother," she replied as she filled her plate. Hogden reached over and lovingly dumped another scoop of food on top.

The next day dawned bright and beautiful. There was an air of excitement throughout the castle as servants bustled about preparing for the wedding. Extra tables were set up in the main dining hall to hold all the food for the wedding feast, and huge baskets of flowers filled the hallways with color and perfume.

Isabella wandered the hallways looking for something to do until the ceremony. Every time she passed a window, she looked out hoping to see the telltale trail of dust in the distance that would mean her parents were arriving. But the few carriages that pulled up belonged to other last minute guests.

She had offered several times to help, but the female servants shooed her away. She spent a little time in the room where Hogitha was getting ready, but after a lengthy conversation about which pair of white shoes Hogitha should wear out of the twenty pairs that had been made for the occasion, Isabella grew restless and left the room. Porkita was expected to help Hogitha, so she was unavailable to keep Isabella company. Grammy was being fitted for a dress for the wedding. The only choice left was to wander the halls, waiting.

A guard found Isabella at the appropriate time and escorted her to a seat in the front of the ballroom next to Grammy. She smiled at Mystic who was standing next to the thrones. Isabella caught her breath at the work the servants had done. There were ribbons and bows everywhere, all pink of course. Great rolls of fine pink silk were draped artfully upon the walls. Not only were there enormous bouquets of pink flowers set around the room, but the floor had been covered in an ankle-deep carpet of soft petals.

As beautiful as the ballroom was, all the chairs set out for guests who wouldn't make it gave it a sad look. When the royal musicians began to play, their song echoed in the emptiness.

Like everyone else, Isabella bowed as King Hamlet and Queen Hogalynn entered and made their way to their thrones. She bowed again as Princess Porcellina, Princess Pigetta, and Princess Porkita glided up the aisle in their finest clothes and jewels. Porkita looked very royal until she drew up next to Isabella and winked.

The music swelled as Hogitha entered the room. Despite her mother's worries that she had lost weight, she looked as though the seams on her gown might burst. Her smile was so wide, it revealed a piece of corn stuck between her teeth, but everyone overlooked it. Isabella felt a lump in her throat as Hogitha floated by, taking up the whole aisle in her white gown of silk and lace. Hogden stood at the front of the room, his face flushed and his ears twitching as she approached. The music ended on a dramatic flourish as the bride and groom faced one another.

A large male in vibrant purple robes bowed to the King and Queen and then stepped before the couple. "Marriage is the joining together of—"

A commotion in the back of the hall caused him to stop. The bride and groom turned toward the noise and the rest of the crowd did the same. Except for Isabella. She stared straight ahead at Hogden and Hogitha, afraid to get her hopes up.

"I'm terribly sorry to disrupt the ceremony, but I just can't wait another moment."

Isabella's head whipped around at the sound of her mother's voice. The world seemed to slow down as she stepped into the aisle and moved toward her parents. She saw her mother's arms reach for her and the tears in her eyes. She didn't see or hear anything else in the room as she flew into her mother's embrace and her father wrapped them both in his strong arms.

Her mother squeezed her so tight, the medallion was crushed between them. The queen pulled away slightly and pointed at the lump she had felt. "What's this?"

"Just a gift from the Lanolions." Her mother pulled her close once more.

After a moment, a grumbly voice behind her said, "I assume these are your parents, Isabella."

Isabella looked through watery eyes to see the King, the Queen, the bride, the groom, and the bride's sisters all beaming at her.

Isabella swallowed the lump in her throat and untangled herself from her parents. "Yes, Your Royal Highness. May I present my parents, King Oscar and Queen Louisa of Grom. Father, Mother, these are our hosts King Hamlet and Queen Hogalynn of Sowden and their daughters. This is Hogitha, who is the bride, and her groom, Hogden. That is Porcellina, and there is Pigetta, and this is my best friend, Porkita."

"Welcome to our home!" King Hamlet said in a booming voice. "We are so honored to meet you at last. We consider your little Isabella to be like one of our own daughters and hope our families will know friendship for many generations."

"Thank you," answered King Oscar. "We have been very anxious to meet you and thank you in person for all you have done for Isabella." The King's voice grew husky as he squeezed Isabella's shoulder. "If it hadn't been for the kindness your family and others showed Isabella, I don't know if she would have had the strength to make it home to us. We are so grateful."

Queen Louisa dabbed at her eyes with a lace handkerchief and said,

"I'm so sorry we interrupted your wedding, Hogitha. I just couldn't wait another minute to see Isabella."

Hogitha wiped her own eyes and answered, "That's perfectly all right. It was worth it to see Isabella smile again. She has been so worried. And our wedding will be even more special now that you are here to share it with us." Queen Louisa gave Hogitha a hug.

King Oscar squeezed Isabella's shoulder again. "We brought you a surprise, Isabella." The guards who had escorted her parents into the room parted to reveal her surprise.

"Lyalus! And Phinius! I'm so glad you are here." She hugged them both. "Thank you, Lyalus, for reaching my father so quickly and warning him about Slyler. And Phinius, I want to hear all about your trip! I have so much to tell you, too."

"Wait until you hear Phinius's story," King Oscar told her. "He led some of the tribes to help round up Rankton's soldiers."

King Hamlet suggested, "Perhaps we should finish the wedding ceremony first, and then we can all get acquainted over the spectacular wedding feast that awaits us. I have heard a lot about both of you, Lyalus and Phinius, and I'm looking forward to talking with you."

Queen Hogalynn took Queen Louisa's arm and escorted her down the aisle to a front row seat. As they walked, Queen Hogalynn said, "I can see that the awful illness that gripped your kingdom has taken its toll on you also. Don't worry, we will fatten you up while you are here, and soon you will be as round and as lovely to look at as you were on your wedding day!" Queen Louisa threw a confused look over her shoulder at Isabella, but Isabella just laughed.

As the others were escorted to their seats, Porkita slipped over to squeeze Isabella's arm. "They are all safe, Isabella. Both our families are here and safe."

Isabella grinned broadly. "Not just our families, Porkita. But everyone I love most. My family, your family, Grammy, Lyalus, Phinius, Mystic, and especially you! All of us together under one roof! I never dreamed this could happen!"

As Princess Isabella walked down the aisle hand in hand with her best friend, she could feel King Tiben's medallion bouncing against her chest. As she looked at the smiling faces of all of her loved ones, she knew they hadn't needed the medallion's magic to beat evil this time. They had just needed each other.

Printed in the United States
17418LVS00001B/55-512